ALISON
the

RULES

BOOKS BY CATHERINE CLARK

TRUTH OR DAIRY
FROZEN RODEO
MAINE SQUEEZE
THE ALISON RULES

the ALISON RULES

CATHERINE CLARK

HARPERTEMPEST

AN *IMPRINT OF* HARPERCOLLINS*PUBLISHERS*

Library of Congress Cataloging-in-Publication Data
Clark, Catherine
    The Alison Rules / Catherine Clark.— 1st ed.
        p.   cm.
    Summary: Alison tries to deal with the pain of her mother's death
by sticking to rules until charming Patrick moves to town, and then
she learns that no matter what, life still happens to you.
    ISBN 0-06-055980-2 — ISBN 0-06-055981-0 (lib. bdg.) [1. Death—
Fiction. 2. Grief—Fiction. 3. Best friends—Fiction. 4. Friendship—
Fiction. 5.   Newspapers—Fiction. 6.   High   schools—Fiction.
7. Schools—Fiction.] I. Title.
PZ7.C5412Al 2004   2003024278
[Fic]—dc22   CIP
                                                            AC

Typography by Andrea Vandergrift
1 2 3 4 5 6 7 8 9 10

First Edition

Many thanks to Abby McAden, Jill Grinberg, Elise Howard, and to the Kristins—Damon, Pederson, and Redman. I'm particularly grateful to Anna Pederson for doing her homework with me, and for telling me that I had to write one more page before I could stop.

CHAPTER ONE

Laurie and I were out in the middle of the river before the Gods could stop us, before they even noticed we were gone.

Back on shore, the Gods were huddled around a bonfire. I was pretty sure that Ryan had been drinking beer that night, or at least he'd smelled a lot like beer when he tried to kiss me. I'd seen Kevin and Paul tossing empty cans into the fire, heard them making bets on which can would melt first.

If Ryan had kissed me this time last year, I'd have kissed him back, I'd have been so happy that I'd be enjoying the kiss and at the same time be dying to tell Laurie about it. But not now. So I wriggled out of his grasp, said, "Cut it out," and ran across the parking lot to get Laurie, who was hanging out with some juniors I didn't know. Laurie didn't know them either, but that didn't stop her the way it stopped me.

We grabbed an old, small aluminum rowboat that had been pulled up on shore and dragged it to the water to make our escape. I never would have stolen someone's rowboat on my own—it was Laurie's idea. Everything was always her idea, including coming down to the boat launch that night, when we hadn't been there in months.

The Gods were Ryan Bouchard, Kevin Calibri, and Paul McGowan. That's what Laurie and I called them because they were like the gods of our school. They were football and hockey superstars, they were good-looking, and they were seniors, two years older than us.

It was bizarre because when Laurie and I were thirteen, it was like they didn't even know we were alive. They never looked at us. We had horrible, intense crushes on them, especially Ryan, but they ignored us, which is probably why we decided they were godlike.

But then all of a sudden, in the spring of freshman year, they wanted to sit next to us at lunch, to invite us down to the launch, to hip check us in the hallway as if we were on the hockey team with them. It could have been spring fever, I guess. But I thought that maybe they'd just suddenly gotten tired of—or run out of—the junior and senior girls. Birch Falls was a small town, and there weren't many potential dates to choose from. You had to be on the lookout for anyone new.

So then sometime last April, Ryan asked me out for ice cream, then to a movie, and I'd panicked and had to ask Laurie to come with me because I didn't know how to act around the Gods on my own. It was okay that I brought

Laurie, though, because Ryan brought Kevin and Paul. I guess none of us were all that good at being alone.

Anyway, that was last year.

We didn't think they were Gods anymore, but it was hard to break the habit of calling them that. The Duds, Laurie called them instead sometimes. Or the Gobs.

"You know I don't actually swim," Laurie said, peering over the bow of the rowboat into the river.

"Yes, you do," I said.

"Not well, anyway," Laurie said.

We both started to laugh. I remembered the last time I saw Laurie dog-paddle in King's Pond. She could hardly stop complaining about how if it was named after a king, it should be a lake or an ocean or at least a sea. She was too busy talking to swim. She ended up inhaling water and then coughing her way from rock to rock.

"But you know what's cool?" Laurie asked. "When you're out here it's like you have no connection to anything. Like we could be almost anywhere right now."

"If we couldn't see the smokestack, yeah." About a half mile downstream you could see the old, closed-down textile mill and the paper company that still functioned—large, long brick buildings. Half the town was dead, and the other half was on life support.

"Let's go back," Laurie said, sounding a little nervous.

"I was actually already trying to do that." I pulled on

the oars to get us headed back toward shore, but the small rowboat kept spinning around, making a circle. I glanced down at the dark, murky water. I knew that I shouldn't be out here. I knew I was supposed to be watching TV or a movie at Laurie's house the way we usually did on Friday nights. We weren't allowed out on our own after dark, except for school events or to go to each other's houses. So we'd lied and invented a Valentine's Day school dance, even though it was a week past Valentine's Day. My father wouldn't notice a detail like that.

"A dance? Really?" my father had said, incredulous. "I thought you hated school dances."

"We're trying to get into the mind-set of a normal person," Laurie had told him. "It starts with going to crap like this."

My father had laughed and agreed I could go, and I'd told him that after the dance I'd be staying over at Laurie's, like I usually did on Friday nights.

It was easy to lie to him. It made me wonder why I didn't start doing it more.

"Alison! We're heading straight for the falls," Laurie said now.

"No, we're not. We're a mile away," I said, exaggerating just a little. "Don't worry, we have time."

But I couldn't steer the boat in the right direction. I'd noticed the oars were slightly different lengths when I slid them into the locks, but that shouldn't matter too much.

I was good with boats, or at least I usually was. My father had insisted on teaching me about the river so I could swim to safety if anything ever happened. He'd had me bail water out of a sinking canoe, tread water for ten minutes, and he taught me how to perform CPR and pump out someone else's lungs in case I was ever boating with my little brother and we capsized, as if my father would let me take Sam out in a boat without going along himself.

I guess because my father sold insurance, he was obsessed with what might happen, what a person needed to be prepared for. I didn't know what he thought would happen, but he probably hadn't expected that I'd be in an old, broken-down rowboat at ten o'clock at night, just to escape Ryan. As far as he knew, I was still *dating* Ryan, I was at the school dance with Ryan, even though it had been over for months now. Dad didn't keep up like he used to, he didn't pay attention anymore.

Laurie shivered and wrapped her arms around herself. She was only wearing a long-sleeved pink T-shirt and jeans and her red suede Vans. At least I had a heavy wool sweater, a turtleneck, and boots. We always dressed for completely different weather, because she was always hot and I was always cold.

"It's freezing out here and we're up a creek without a paddle," Laurie said.

"No, we're up a river with two oars," I corrected her. "They're just two different lengths and they don't work.

5

That's what you get for stealing someone's boat, I guess."

"*Borrowing*. Not stealing. Hey, see those lights? Way back there?" Laurie pointed to the shore. "*That's* the bon-fire."

"I know."

"It's getting really far away."

"I know."

"Give it a little more muscle."

I set the oars on my thighs and pushed a loose strand of hair out of my eyes. My wispy, shoulder-length hair refused to stay in any barrette or holder I owned. "Do you want to try?"

"Come on," Laurie urged. "Please. This is making me kind of nervous."

Laurie, nervous. That was something unusual. It sort of scared me to realize we actually weren't all that safe right now.

I tilted the mismatched oars so that I could see the blades in the moonlight. Then I slid the oars back through the locks and scooted forward on the tiny benchlike seat in the boat. I pulled as hard as I could. The oarlocks screeched as the metal oar and lock scraped against each other, then suddenly there was a loud snap on the left side. I reached out to catch the lock, but it splashed into the river before I could grab it.

Laurie screamed, reaching overboard and fishing around in the water with her hands for the broken lock. "It sank," she said. "It's sleeping with the fishes. Now what?"

"Let's each take an oar and paddle. I'll steer," I said, handing Laurie the shorter oar.

"You're so calm in an emergency. I hate that about you." Laurie started to paddle. "This is the worst canoe trip I've ever been on. I want you to know that."

"This isn't a canoe," I said.

"Same difference." She shivered. "This is even worse than the time I went fishing with my dad when I was six. It was awful."

"I was *there*," I reminded her.

"Oh. Right. Yeah, you caught a bunch of fish. I tried not to throw up."

"Don't throw up now. Please don't—" I stopped as I heard a boat coming toward us. I could make out a small green light on its starboard side.

"Who's that?" Laurie asked. "Is that the coast guard?"

"This isn't the coast," I said, laughing.

"Oh, god. We're in so much trouble," Laurie said. "My mother's going to *kill* me."

The boat's engine revved, the bow bouncing on the water, carving the river as it plowed ahead. A large headlight on the front of the boat shone in my eyes.

"You know what? I bet it's the Gobs. Coming to get us," Laurie said.

The boat sped toward us, and I felt myself grip the oar even more tightly. "Do they see us? What if they don't see us? What if they're drunk and they don't—"

"Here, I have some matches!" Laurie dropped the oar in the bottom of the boat and rifled through her pockets.

"Why do you have matches?" I asked as Laurie frantically tried to get one lit and I kept an eye on the approaching boat.

"I stole them from Mom so she couldn't smoke tonight." Mrs. Kuzmuskus had been trying to quit for the past year, but it seemed as if she was smoking even more than before.

"Doesn't she have a lighter?" I asked. "Or she'll just use the stove or something."

"Yeah, I know, I thought of that. She can light it a thousand different ways, but at least this makes her *think* about it first. That's the genius of it."

"Hey. Hey!" I yelled, standing up as the boat came nearer, not slowing down. I waved my arms in the air.

"Alison! It's gonna ram—"

At the last second, the boat whirled around us, and we both watched as it made a wide circle and came back at us, going slower now. I heard loud voices, then laughing and Ryan shouting to Kevin to catch our boat the next time they went past.

"I knew it was them," Laurie said. "Losers."

The motorboat came to a stop beside us. Ryan was sitting in the back by the motor, steering, and Kevin and Paul were sitting in the middle on a small bench seat.

8

"Hey. Need a lift?" Kevin stood up and reached out to grab the rowboat as they cruised slowly past us, but he stumbled, bumping into the side of the boat. "Whoa," he said, falling back onto the bench seat.

"No, but I think *you* do," Laurie said.

"Shut up, Kuzmuskus," Kevin said, slurring her last name into an unrecognizable jumble.

Ryan circled back around, and this time Paul leaned out over the bow to grab the rowboat as Ryan cut the motor. They slowly drifted up to us. "What the hell are you guys doing out here?" Paul asked.

"We're on a cruise. What do you think?" Laurie said as Paul threaded a thick rope through the ring in the prow of the rowboat and knotted it so they could tow us back to shore.

"That you're insane?" Paul laughed at us.

"That you shouldn't be out here. That you don't know what you're doing." Ryan said, looking intently at me.

"Well, sure, but what *took* you so long?" Laurie said. "We could have frozen to death out here."

"Next time, I'll go out with you," Ryan said as he and Paul pulled the bow of the rowboat up onto shore ten minutes later, with me still sitting in it. "You shouldn't have tried that by yourselves."

I glanced at Ryan's face as I quickly climbed out of the rowboat, one foot landing in the water and the other on mud. "We didn't need you this time," I said.

"Yeah, right. You were totally drifting. You were hopeless against the current," Paul said. He could be kind of a know-it-all, which had always bothered me. He was the quarterback on the football team, so he was used to telling people what to do.

"That's only because the oarlock broke. We would have made it back," Laurie said. She hated being told what she could or couldn't do. "We were paddling back and we were doing fine."

Paul just laughed and shook his head. "Yeah, okay. Sure thing, Kuzmuskus."

"Listen. The day we have to rely on you guys—especially you?" Laurie reached out and pushed her finger against Kevin's chest. "We're in serious trouble."

Kevin put his arm around Laurie's shoulders and squeezed her as if he were about to wrestle her to the ground. "You're funny. You know that, right, Kuzmuskus?" He sounded sort of offended but also impressed by her. Laurie could say anything to anybody. She wasn't afraid of them. She wasn't afraid of anything.

"Yeah, I know," she said. "I'm freaking hilarious. Come on, Alison, let's go."

"Will you guys put the boat back under that tree?" I asked, pointing to where we'd found it.

"Sure. But wait up—you need a ride home, right?" Ryan asked.

"No, thanks. We'll walk," Laurie said.

"Don't be stupid. It's late," Ryan said.

"We're not being stupid. You guys are wasted," Laurie pointed out. "You shouldn't even have been driving the boat."

"They are. I'm not," Ryan said.

"Yeah. Well. We'll still take our chances walking."

Ryan came closer to me. "You look cold. You want my jacket?" He shrugged out of his letter jacket, which was covered with gold pins for football and hockey. I thought of all the times I'd worn that jacket. And the last time I'd worn it, clutching the scratchy wool fabric against my face, trying to burrow inside, trying to bury myself in it.

"I'm not cold," I said. I had been shivering a little, but I stopped. "Anyway, we have to go. Thanks for the tow."

"Anytime." Ryan smiled at me, and for a second I remembered why I'd once thought he was so cute. He had those really deep blue eyes, those killer cheekbones, that perfect nose. Last year this would have been the most meaningful thing that had ever happened to me. Last year I would have been turning cartwheels or doing something embarrassing like that to show how happy I was.

I turned and started walking beside Laurie up from the boat launch to the main road.

"We should have made them give us Ryan's truck," she said.

I laughed. "Yeah, but we don't drive."

"How hard can it be? If we can drive a boat, we can drive a car."

"But we've never driven a boat," I reminded her. "Not the kind with an engine."

"You always get hung up on technicalities. My mom lets me steer sometimes in the morning, while she puts on her mascara. I mean, that's practice." She rubbed her arms. "Notice how Ryan didn't offer me his jacket. You know, he really likes you, still. Why didn't you let him drive us home? I mean, what's wrong with him?"

"I don't know. Nothing," I said. "He just . . . he bores me, that's all."

I couldn't tell her that it wasn't what was wrong with him. That it was me.

Then again, maybe she already knew.

Mrs. Kuzmuskus was laughing at something on TV when we walked in. "Hey, where have you guys been?" she asked.

"Nowhere, Mom. Just hanging out," Laurie replied. "Mom. It smells fruity in here. What did you do?"

"I bought some of that orange oil cleaning stuff. I was trying to get ahead on the Saturday cleaning." Mrs. K.—as I called her—pushed back the headband she wore to hold her curly, permed hair off her face. She was wearing a blue velour hooded sweatshirt and jeans. "Trapped in the seventies" was how Laurie described her.

"No, you were covering up the smell of smoke. Weren't you?" Laurie asked.

"No, I was not doing anything like that. I was cleaning," Mrs. K. insisted. "So we won't have to do very much at all tomorrow."

I always went to Laurie's house on Friday nights, and Laurie and Mrs. K. always cleaned the house together on Saturday mornings after we all had pancakes and bacon and coffee. It wasn't much of a routine, but it was something to do. Lately Laurie and I had started drinking coffee, too, which was a problem because whenever Mrs. K. smelled coffee, it made her want to smoke. She had to quit one to quit the other, which was why it wasn't working out for her yet.

We hurried past the sofa so Mrs. K. wouldn't see our muddy, wet pant legs. If she found out we'd been out on the river, she'd be livid. She was convinced that the river was filled with chemicals that were poisoning us all. If there were another decent-paying job in town for her besides working at the Riverbank Paper Company, right beside the river, she'd take it—but there wasn't. We were a one-company kind of town.

I went into the guest room and quickly changed into my pajamas—a short white T-shirt that used to be Sam's when he was about nine and a pair of striped green lounge pants. I took the barrette out of my hair, brushed the tangles out, and grabbed a red baseball cap from the hook on the wall in Laurie's room.

"So, was it fun? Whatever it was that you did?" Mrs. K. asked when we went back into the living room.

"It was . . . interesting," Laurie said.

Her mother looked at me and raised an eyebrow. "Care to explain?"

"We ran into Ryan tonight," I said. "And Kevin and Paul." I decided to leave out the part where we were drifting helplessly in the river current. She wouldn't like that.

Mrs. K. sighed. "I really wish you wouldn't spend so much time with those guys."

"Mom," Laurie said. "They're not evil."

"Anyway, we don't. Spend much time with them," I said. "Hardly at all anymore."

"Not since Alison decided to kick Ryan to the curb," Laurie added. "Not that we have curbs here."

Mrs. K. looked at me. "Just as well."

"And you don't have to worry about them and *me*, because they don't even think I'm a girl." Laurie tossed a pillow into the air, caught it, then tossed it again. "They all drool over Alison, the blond goddess, but it's like—they just punch me and call me Kuzmuskus like I'm one of their hockey buddies."

"That's because they're jerks," I said. "They're Gobs. They're Duds."

"True." She caught the pillow and grinned at me.

"You know what? They're not *good* enough for you. They're too stupid to see how great you are. That's the problem."

"Mom. *Mom.* Stop. Don't even tell me it's about personality and not looks," Laurie said.

"Okay, fine." Mrs. K. cleared her throat. "Alison? I saw your father at the store tonight."

"When you went to buy smokes?" Laurie said.

"Nooooo, when I went to buy groceries." She sprayed the TV screen with Windex. "He looked tired. Do you think he's sleeping all right?"

"Sure," I said, while I tried to remember what he'd looked like that morning when I passed him in the kitchen on my way out. In a way, I didn't really keep track of him any more than he kept track of me. "You know what? You missed a spot," I said to Mrs. K., pointing at a smudge on the TV screen. Then I realized what an obnoxious thing that was to say. "Sorry."

CHAPTER TWO

We met Patrick in geometry class three days later. Mr. Lewis, our teacher with the military flair, practically had him stand and salute as he introduced him on Monday morning.

"Kirk, Patrick?" Mr. Lewis called in a deep voice, sounding like the army lieutenant he used to be, or at least sounding the way army lieutenants were portrayed on TV—I wouldn't know what they were like in real life. Mr. Lewis wore a crisp, wrinkle-free white shirt and a tie that looked tight enough to choke him every single day, even on casual Fridays, which he apparently hadn't gotten the gist of yet.

"Here," a voice answered.

I turned around and saw a boy sitting in the back of the room, near the window. He had very short, thick, sandy-brown hair that almost stood up in spikes. He had freckles and looked as if he'd been spending time at the beach, which didn't make sense since it was late February and a few chunks of gray icy slush still littered the ground. He wore a dark blue T-shirt with a surf logo on it and faded baggy jeans, and I wondered if he had moved here from somewhere warm, like Florida. I felt sorry for him, if he had. Birch Falls was going to be so boring in comparison. Western Massachusetts had nothing on Miami.

"Stand up, please," Mr. Lewis said.

Now everyone turned to look at him. He was tall—maybe six feet—and thin. Even though I was looking at him, too, I almost wished I wasn't. Because I knew how that felt, having twenty-three people fix their eyes on you and not let go for a minute. I hated it. You felt like a butterfly pinned up for display.

But it was such a curious thing to have a transfer this late in the term that we couldn't help ourselves. We were dying for a fresh face, for a pattern we hadn't seen before.

Mr. Lewis politely said, "Welcome. We're glad to have you."

"Thanks," the boy said, nodding.

"Keaney, Kirk, Kuzmuskus," Mr. Lewis muttered as he ticked off the desks in front of him. "I haven't had three Ks since the Kozontkoski triplets." He sounded annoyed, as if we had chosen our last names as a personal affront to him. He insisted on having order in his classroom. He'd been teaching at Birch Falls Regional High for twenty-five years, and his alphabetical seating chart was legendary—historic, even. "They'll frame his seating charts after he's gone," Laurie had said once, "and that'll be his legacy, which is really, really sad, because he's actually not a bad teacher."

"Well, as long as we can all alphabetize," Laurie now

17

said under her breath to me. "I mean, that *is* what we're here for."

"Son, come up and sit right here," Mr. Lewis commanded. He walked to my desk and rapped it with his knuckles.

I looked up at Mr. Lewis. No, I thought. Did he really expect me to move? Up until now the alphabet had worked out just right. Laurie and I got to sit next to each other and I could ask her for help with my proofs. I needed a lot of help. The Pythagorean theorem was wasted on me. Theorems, in general, were wasted on me. Mr. Lewis had told us that geometry was based on postulates, because you couldn't prove everything and therefore had to rely on assumptions that were generally accepted.

That didn't work for me. I was good at memorizing facts—history, grammar, multiplication tables. Facts were easy and made sense. Postulates weren't and didn't.

"You know, does it really matter if we all sit in order?" Laurie asked. "Why not have the new guy just sit anywhere, and we'll all know—Hey, that's the new guy!"

"Actually, I prefer Patrick," the boy said to Laurie as he moved up the aisle toward us. "Not 'new guy.' Thanks."

"I thought your name was Kirk," Laurie said, looking up at him. "Kirk Patrick."

"No, it's Patrick," he said.

"Patrick Kirkpatrick. Wow." Laurie shook her head and her long, dark brown hair swirled around her shoulders. "What a mouthful."

"No. It's Patrick *Kirk*, not Kirkpatrick," he corrected her, more annoyed now.

Mr. Lewis loudly cleared his throat. "Young man, don't let Ms. *Kuzmuskus* give you a hard time about your name."

Patrick looked at Laurie and grinned. "I'm so sorry. ''Cause must kiss'?" he said. "Interesting."

Laurie frowned at him. She was used to teasing other people, not being made fun of—she'd usually do that before giving anyone else a chance. "No, Kuzmuskus. Look, never mind," she said, curling her hair around her ear, the way she did whenever she was nervous.

Mr. Lewis clapped his hands together. "Chop-chop, Alison. Get your things and move. Everyone, *adjust*."

We all shuffled desks, and I glanced over at Laurie as I sat down. I hoped Patrick was as good at geometry as she was. I needed some help from someone. I was next to the window now, so no one was on that side of me, and I had fewer opportunities to borrow answers. I was someone who needed other people's answers. Desperately.

"So. What are we working on? Hyperteneuse triangles?" Patrick asked me.

"Did you just say 'hyperteneuse'? Because it's the hy*pot*enuse," Laurie told him. "And it's not a triangle."

"Okay. Sure." Patrick opened his textbook, clutched his spiky hair with his hands, and leaned down toward the desk as if he were in despair.

That pose looked familiar. It looked sort of like me.

Mr. Lewis started handing out sheets of paper to each

19

of us. "Today is the first Monday of the month, and you know what that means."

"Buy one pizza, get the second one for a dollar?" Patrick muttered under his breath.

I smiled, glad to know he had a sense of humor. He'd need it, in this class, in this town.

"Not quite," Laurie said. "Pop quiz. He calls it pop, but we have them the first and third Mondays of every month. Regularly scheduled quiz would be more like it." She leaned over toward him and caught my eye as she did. "But don't worry. You know all about corresponding parts, right?"

I smiled as Patrick gave first Laurie a confused look and then me. When we first started geometry and Mr. Lewis talked about the sum of corresponding parts, Laurie and I couldn't stop laughing whenever he said that. It was the term our instructor had used in our health sciences class years ago to describe the male and female anatomy.

"I know nothing, actually," Patrick said as he rummaged in a yellow courier-type bag.

Laurie tried to hand him a pencil.

"No, I only work in pen," he said.

"But this is math," Laurie said. "What about mistakes?"

Mr. Lewis clapped his hands together. "I hear talking. I should hear writing."

I reached into my backpack and fished out an extra pen, which I handed to Patrick. Then I stared at the quiz for a few seconds, until an office assistant walked into our classroom and talked to Mr. Lewis. She came over and handed me a typed note on school stationery:

```
Alison,
This is not an emergency.
But please report to my office immediately.
Thank you.
Mr. Cucklowicz
```

Mr. Cucklowicz was the school guidance counselor. Due to the sound of his last name we all referred to him as "Kook," as in "cuckoo." It was such a good and obvious nickname that he didn't even mind being called Coach Kook by his wrestling team.

I quickly stuffed my geometry book into my bag, wondering why I had to be in his office "immediately" if it wasn't an emergency. He should know not to scare me like that. What was going on? I glanced across Patrick's desk at Laurie and whispered the word "Kook" before I stood up. I dropped the note on Laurie's desk as I walked past, so she'd know what was up. Whatever Kook wanted, it couldn't be good. He didn't summon you for praise or great news.

"Hurry back. The quiz anxiously awaits your return. And you can't afford to miss much, Ms. Keaney," Mr. Lewis said as he handed me a hall pass.

There's nothing like getting a vote of confidence from your teacher when you're struggling.

• • •

"How've you been, Alison?" Mr. Cucklowicz said when I sat down in his office and he closed the door behind me.

When Kook sat down in his desk chair, he was about as tall as he was standing up, because he had the shortest legs I'd ever seen on a man—on anyone, really. He was still probably the fittest guidance counselor in the state. Being the wrestling coach, he almost always wore sweatpants and various polyester fitness clothes. I lived in fear of ever seeing him in his stretchy nylon wrestling getup. Once, Laurie and I were leaving the gym when he was walking in and we sprinted out the door, laughing and shielding our eyes.

I'd only seen Kook in a dress suit—a jacket and tie—once. He looked apelike, with giant broad shoulders, long arms, and short legs. That made him a good wrestler, I guess, but a funny-looking man.

"I'm okay," I told him, shifting in the chair.

"Really? But you haven't responded to any of my notes."

"Notes?" I asked. What was he talking about? On the bookcase behind him, a small black radio was playing loud classical music, and he reached over to turn down the volume. He blared music like that at wrestling practice, to motivate people or to motivate himself. It was handy because if we heard the music, we knew to stay away from the gym.

Kook turned back to me with a curious smile. Why was he smiling at me like that? What did he want? "I've been leaving notes inside your locker for the past two weeks, requesting you drop by my office for a meeting," he said. "So why haven't you come by?"

I stared at the framed diplomas on the wall behind him, certifying his psychology degrees. One of the frames was hanging crookedly. "Actually, I didn't know you wanted to see me, because I don't use my locker," I said; and as soon as I did, I regretted it. I was confessing something he could take and run with.

"Oh?" He stared at my large red backpack on the linoleum floor beside my chair. "You don't use your school locker? Why?"

As far as I could tell, from my previous visits, "Why is that?" and "Why?" and "Why not?" formed the basis of his deep and probing psychological approach.

"Alison. Your locker," Kook said again. "You said you don't use it? Why is that?"

"I just don't," I said.

"Yes, I realize that. But why not?" he said.

"I just—I don't. Would you stop asking that? I mean, why. Why anything? Does there have to be a reason for everything?"

"No, there doesn't have to be," Kook said. "But there usually is."

"I don't know about that," I said. Things happening without reasons was becoming a theme lately. And it was completely irrational, which is why I wouldn't tell Kook about it. But I had decided that if I didn't go back to using my locker, maybe everything would stay okay for a while. I had ways of doing things now that I couldn't change. Things were set now. They weren't perfect, they weren't even good, but they were set. That included not using my locker.

"So have you had a problem at your locker?" Kook asked. "Have you had problems with break-ins? Do you need a new locker assignment or a new lock? Because we can go talk to maintenance—"

"No, it's not that. It works . . . fine," I said, though I wouldn't really know, would I? Anyway, even though I wasn't using it now, I didn't want it taken away, reassigned. "Look, maybe someday that horrible smell from the chemistry lab in the hallway across from it will seem like a good thing," I said.

Kook stared at me, as if I weren't supposed to be making jokes. For some reason that made me babble even more.

"The thing is that I'd really just rather carry my stuff with me most of the time," I went on. "But once in a while, I'll use my locker, so. It's fine."

"Oh, well, okay. To each her own, I suppose." He cleared his throat. "Listen, Alison. Are you all right?" he asked. "How are things?"

"Fine," I said, because that's what everyone always wanted to hear.

"You've got a B minus average right now, which is acceptable, I guess. Not quite up to your potential, but sophomore year's a struggle for a lot of people."

I just stared at him.

Kook nodded. "Well. It's been six months, and the reason I've been anxious to talk to you is that I wanted to know how you're coping."

Six months. Had it been that long? Sometimes it felt like it had only been a week ago; some days it felt like years. The way Kook said it made me feel terrible, as if I'd missed someone's birthday, an important anniversary. Or maybe I was just guilty because he was keeping track of the months and I wasn't.

But I knew his concern wasn't sincere. He was only asking me how I was because he had a little prompt in his computer that flagged the date, and my name popped up with the words: SIX MONTHS; CHECK ON ALISON KEANEY. This was his job. They paid him to keep track of us. They paid him to use words like "coping."

"This is the standard check, right?" I said.

"What do you mean?"

"I mean, next come the questions about whether I'm sleeping well at night and whether I'm eating right and if I am, why is that, and if I'm not, then why not."

"Alison, relax. It's nothing like *that*," Kook said. He tapped the ends of his fingers together. "I'm just concerned. If there's anything you want to talk about . . . I'm here."

"Thanks." If I wanted to talk, which I didn't, the last person I'd choose was Mr. Cucklowicz. He had to know that, didn't he? The fact he had to summon me to his office should give him a clue.

"So. Are you staying involved—are you doing any new extracurricular activities? Joining any teams?"

I had to give him a good answer so he'd decide I was all right and leave me alone. I had to tell him what he wanted to hear, which was that I'd responded to his urging and "gotten involved." "Yes, actually, I am," I said. "I'm working on the *Bugle* now. As a news reporter. Well, as *the* news reporter."

"That's right, I saw your name in a byline. Well, that must be fun." Kook smiled at me.

"Sort of," I said. "I mean, yes. It is fun."

There was a long, awkward pause. I could either wait for him to comment on my mental condition some more, or I could tell him I wanted to be the first girl on the wrestling team, or I could try to escape. "Well, I have to get back to class, okay? We have quizzes in geometry every other Monday and today's one of those Mondays, so . . . "

"Of course. You're excused." Kook handed me another hall pass. "But keep in touch, Alison, all right?"

"Yes. Definitely. I'll definitely keep in touch," I said. As much as I usually did, which wasn't promising a thing.

When I got back to class, quiz time was over and Laurie was standing at the blackboard, chalk in hand, solving a proof for the class. I flashed her a smile and went to my seat. Mr. Lewis always gave Laurie the most difficult problems and then he'd get excited when she solved them. It was like a dare he kept issuing and she never backed down. It was a good strategy, since Laurie liked dares. Sometimes Mr. Lewis acted as if she was going to make him famous one day, because he'd discovered the next math genius, because Laurie would put him and Birch Falls on the map. Or at least on more maps than we were now, which wouldn't be difficult.

I nearly hit Patrick with my bag as I swung it off my shoulder to set it on the floor.

"Caution, as overhead items may have shifted during the flight," he said, ducking his head.

I looked over at him and smiled. "Sorry."

"That's okay. Please hit me. Knock me on the head. Take me out of my misery. I'm begging you," he whispered.

Laurie came back from the board just in time to hear him and she stared at the two of us, wondering what was going on, what we were talking about. "You're begging her? Already?" she asked. "You have to work up to that. That's one of the Alison rules."

"Alison rules?" Patrick repeated.

"Yeah. Don't worry—you'll find out," Laurie said.

I wanted to tell him it was ridiculous, that I didn't have a set of rules. That it was just something Laurie said.

Laurie sniffed the air, leaning closer to him. "What's that fruit smell? Like . . . sour something."

"Apple. Want one?" Patrick reached into an outside

pocket of his yellow courier bag and held out a big handful of Jolly Ranchers to her.

"No, thanks. Lewis will kill you if he catches you eating candy in here," she told him.

"Somehow I think I'll live," Patrick said. "Unfortunately." He glanced over at me and smiled, holding out his hands, the candy spilling into both. "Lemon, cherry, apple, or watermelon."

I just stared at them for a second, trying to decide which flavor I wanted.

"Take 'em all," he said, putting a dozen or so candies on my desk. "Go wild."

I stared at them for a second before getting out my notebook. Watermelon was Sam's favorite so I took one to take home. I opened a cherry one and put it in my mouth. I tried to put the rest back on Patrick's desk

"No, it's okay, keep 'em," Patrick whispered. "We've got like ten more hours to get through." He smiled at me. "Give or take two years."

I divided the flavors, pushing them around my desk, making rows.

3 lemon, 4 cherry, 2 apple, 2 watermelon.

6 months.

CHAPTER THREE

"You guys again?" Patrick asked as we walked into journalism class. It wasn't held in a typical classroom. There were a couple of large tables pushed together to form a rectangle and behind them, against the windows, long tables with computers and a big printer.

"Hey. Nice to see you, too," Laurie said.

"Hi," I said.

Patrick tilted his chair back against the radiator, and propped one foot on the table. "Am I in the right place?" he asked.

"That depends," Laurie said. "Do you like endless boredom? If so, then this school is the right place for you."

"No, actually, I meant for the school newspaper. Is this the right room?" Patrick asked.

I nodded. "Check it out." I pointed to the old framed front pages of the *Birch Falls High Bugle* on one wall.

"But the paper's the least boring thing about this place," Laurie said, "so you know, if you can't handle it and you want to get back to the endless boredom, there's

29

probably a chess club meeting you could attend—"

"Hey, I just *moved* from endless boredom. In fact, that was the name of the place. Had it on the license plates." Patrick formed the shape of a rectangle with his hands and drew a line across the bottom of it. "The Endless Boredom State."

"Uh-huh. Right," Laurie said, and I laughed.

"So where did you move here from?" I asked him.

"Maine."

"Maine? Maine's not boring," Laurie said. "What are you talking about? I love Maine."

"You've been to Maine?" I turned to her. "When did you go to Maine?"

"Last summer. My mom and I did that road trip, remember?"

I hadn't remembered. It must have been the end of last summer, which was sort of a blur to me. I'd worked at the I-C Treat, as many hours as I could get, and we hadn't taken any family trips.

"Maine—the way life should be," Laurie went on. "Or at least that's what those blue signs on the turnpike say."

"Oh, sure. Maine, the way life should be," Patrick said. "You know who thinks that? People from New Hampshire. That's it."

I laughed. "Hey, we're practically *in* New Hampshire, so watch what you say."

Patrick looked at me, confused. "I thought we were almost in Vermont."

"Same difference." Laurie tapped the table in front of Patrick. "So . . . I'm sorry, I don't get it. You're from the freezing cold north. How can you have a tan?" she asked.

"Easy. We just went to South Carolina on spring break," Patrick said. "Dad played golf, I did not."

"Why not?" Laurie asked.

"'Cause . . . I hate golf?" Patrick said. "Because I can't stand trying to hit a little white ball with eighteen different clubs, and golf shirts are hideous, and I'd have to listen to my dad make small talk, and watch him hit on the cart girls, and tell me I should be more like Tiger Woods?"

"Oh. I see. Well, as long as you're not bitter." Laurie turned to me and smiled.

A few more people came into the room—Jason Lawrence, the sports editor, and Dave Perkins, the managing editor—but so far our teacher hadn't showed.

"Hey, while we're waiting for the big cheeses, you want to look it over? Here are some of my best columns." Laurie grabbed a stack of papers and handed them to Patrick. "They're actually all good, so. Just randomly read."

Patrick raised an eyebrow. "As long as you're not vain."

Laurie had her own editorial column called "Kuz Why?" In it she asked "the important, burning questions of our time," or so she said. For example, some of her recent topics were things like: Why are the graduation requirements so rigid? Why can't we just take the subjects we're interested in? Why is there no creative writing department? Why can't we revise the dress code? Why can't we have school field trips more often? Why won't the bullies shut up? Why do the budget cuts need to be so deep? Et cetera. We all knew that she would probably win awards when we went to the New England high school newspaper conference in April.

Me, I wasn't nearly as creative, so I stuck with the somewhat boring topic of school news. As I said earlier, I am good at dealing with facts. And if things ever happened at our school, school news wouldn't be such a bad assignment. But it usually involved reporting on school board meetings, debate contests, and new office equipment. I didn't have to write long stories, but I got the front page. It was a nice arrangement. They were pieces that I supposedly could clip and put in my portfolio, Mr. Garcia said. At this point, I had no idea what I was ever going to do with said portfolio. But maybe the clips would offset some of the things I wasn't so good at—like geometry—in the college-application scales.

The Birch Falls High Bugle was printed in large letters on the first page, and then, underneath it, REFLECTING RIVERBANK PAPER PRIDE. Riverbank Paper sponsored the newspaper, so they got to brag about themselves. The banner of the school newspaper nearly took up half the front page, which made it easy for me to fill the rest with news. Since we didn't have much news, this was important. I couldn't imagine how I'd stretch out an article about new first-aid kits in the nurse's office to more than a paragraph.

"So. I have a question." Patrick scooted his chair over to the bookcase beside the radiator and grabbed a newspaper from one of the shelves. "What's a 'high bugle'?"

Laurie and I both laughed. "I don't know, but I think it's better than a low bugle," I said.

"Okay, Patrick Kirkpatrick, I have a question for you," Laurie said.

He set down the newspapers and put his hands behind his head. "Shoot."

"Why did you move here now? I mean, the end of February is kind of a strange time to transfer."

"Yeah, no doubt. Well, see, you know Riverbank Paper, right? My dad—"

"He moved here to work there?" Laurie interrupted. "You know, my mom works there."

"Really?" Patrick looked around the table. "I know this is probably a really dumb question. But does *everyone* in this town work there?"

"Almost," Laurie said.

"My dad sells insurance," I said, before he could ask. We exchanged a sort of awkward look. "So, not *quite* everyone."

"Still, Patrick Kirkpatrick. I don't get it," Laurie said. "You just moved here, and you want to work on the *High Bugle*? I mean, Alison's lived here for her entire *life* and she's only just now getting involved."

Patrick just stared at me for a couple of seconds.

"You're slow. That's all I can think."

"Seriously," Laurie said, and the three of us were laughing. "What are you doing here?"

Patrick looked a little confused. "Do you want me to leave?"

"No! No, not at all. I didn't mean it like that. Sorry. I just wondered, you know, why."

Patrick crumpled an empty plastic candy wrapper in his hand. "Well, the thing is that my dad doesn't exactly work at the company. I mean, he does, but not the way you're thinking. He actually just got hired to run it."

"Ohhhh," Laurie said. "I get it. You *have* to work on the paper because you're like the son of the Riverbank Paper Pride."

"Son of the pride. Wasn't that a movie?" Patrick asked.

Mr. Garcia walked into the room then, with Kelley Moroney, the editor in chief. Mr. Garcia was wearing a shirt and tie, khaki pants, and a pair of black shoes with tan leather trim that looked straight out of a bowling alley— but a more urban, hip alley than the Birch Bowl. He had a huge selection of cool shoes that wouldn't really be cool on anyone else, but they looked good on him. "He's a shoe god," Laurie had said, and she'd told me that he always went to Boston to buy them, and she'd memorized the names of the cool stores where he went. Laurie knew a lot about Mr. Garcia. She was half in love with Mr. Garcia, actually.

"Not in that way-too-old-for-me Vladimir Nabokov *Lolita* way, not at all," she'd insisted when she'd tried to explain her feelings to me. "I just know he's the greatest teacher I've ever had and probably ever will have." That was how she'd convinced me to work on the *Bugle*—by going on and on about how much fun it was to work with Mr. Garcia. That and the fact Kook was breathing down my neck for me to "get involved."

And Laurie turned out to be right. Mr. Garcia could light up a room, as the saying goes. He could make you think, and laugh, and want to work on things. Mr. Garcia pushed people to write better, and take better photographs, and even to choose better fonts. He wrote with expensive fountain pens, had a huge library of books that he let students borrow, and was the one teacher at Birch Falls who simply refused to coach anything, no matter how hard they begged him to take over the track team or revamp the volleyball squad. He just didn't care about that, about being well-rounded. He took us out to eat sometimes, instead. He considered that an extracurricular.

"And you are?" Mr. Garcia said as he looked around the table at the staff and noticed Patrick sitting there.

Patrick sat up a little straighter. "Patrick Kirk."

"Kirkpatrick," Laurie added.

Mr. Garcia glanced at her, seemed to be confused, and then turned back to him. "Hello . . . Patrick. I'm glad you're here."

"Thanks," Patrick said. "It's nice to meet you, Mr. Garcia." He waved at the rest of the newspaper staff. "Hey, everyone."

"So, you just transferred here?" Mr. Garcia sat on the edge of the table, near Patrick. "Where were you before this?"

Patrick tapped a pen against the table. "Well, it's sort of a long story. I mean, a private school. It's really small. You've probably never heard of it. But I'm here now."

"You certainly are," Laurie said. "And you have our sympathy."

"Ignore her," Mr. Garcia told Patrick. "*We've* all learned to." He smiled at Laurie. "Okay. Well, did you work on a school newspaper, wherever it is you used to be?"

"Yeah. What can you actually *do*?" Kelley asked.

Patrick looked at her, seeming a little taken aback.

"You know, Mr. Garcia, we really need someone else in sports," Jason said. Our sports section was sometimes two pages long—which was a lot, considering the paper was only four total. There wasn't much else to do but join a team or get excited about rooting for one.

"Oh. Well, that's cool. But I'm not that interested in sports writing," Patrick said.

"Neither am I. Great men think alike. I've been trying to downsize that section for years." Mr. Garcia smiled. "We'll find something else for you, don't worry. We never turn away anyone who wants to go into journalism."

"Very noble of you," Patrick commented.

"Oh, we're *extremely* noble," Laurie said. "We're constantly getting awards for that. Pulitzer Prizes—"

"*Nobel* Prizes," Patrick said.

Laurie nodded, laughing. "Exactly." She gave me a look, like *do you believe this?* It was strange, how they seemed to have the same sense of humor.

"So let me introduce everyone and we'll talk about what you might like to do," Mr. Garcia said. "This is our editor in chief, Kelley Moroney."

Kelley gave Patrick a very tight smile, as if she hadn't wanted to, but she was doing it for politeness' sake. It was difficult having Kelley as editor in chief, because she didn't like anyone who didn't do things her way. But she was also the one willing to work the hardest, so she sort of deserved the job. She was a junior and was also the yearbook editor, and she probably ran clubs that I didn't even know existed. She held the attendance record and had never been late to school, as far as I knew, not even in blinding snowstorms. "She's one of those big-fish-in-a-small-pond people," Laurie had said when Kelley got the editor in chief job. "When she leaves here, she'll be nobody and she won't be able to deal with it. So let her be in charge now." We thought it was the best and worst: to work with Mr. Garcia, we had to work with Kelley.

"And this is Dave, our managing editor," Mr. Garcia continued. He went around the table, pointing out each one of us. "This is Alison, school news. Laurie, whose editorial column, 'Kuz Why?' is legendary around here. In her mind, anyway."

"Oh. You're hurting me. You're killing me," Laurie said.

"In sports, there's Jason. We have two photographers—Aleyta and Connor. Our layout is done by Shannon, proofreading by Erica. And that about rounds out our illustrious staff." Mr. Garcia picked up a clipboard. "So. Anything appeal to you, Patrick?"

"I was thinking maybe a lifestyle or arts and entertainment section. You know, movie reviews, CD releases, books," Patrick suggested.

"I handle all the entertainment news," Kelley said.

Patrick just stared at her with a surprised look on his face. I knew what he was thinking: Kelley didn't seem fun enough to write about entertainment.

"But . . . you could use some help, couldn't you?" Laurie asked her. "I mean, there's way more we could put into that section. We're missing a lot of movie releases."

"And that's because they're R rated and not suitable for us." Kelley smoothed the back of her short, blond-highlighted hair. She was a little on the uptight side.

"And that's also because a movie has never actually opened here," Dave added. "We get stuff a couple of weeks late, usually," he explained to Patrick.

Patrick's eyes widened, as if he was just realizing how

stranded he was, whereas the rest of us already knew. "Well, how about a gossip column then?" he suggested. "Reporting on who was seen where and with whom."

I pictured Patrick with a tiny reporter's notepad, following people around town, sitting in diners and bars and the town square, looking for Birch Falls dirt. He'd probably find a lot.

"I don't know, Patrick. I don't think it'd be that interesting. And if it was too interesting, we'd get into trouble." Mr. Garcia tapped the desk with a black and silver fountain pen.

"Like Jason said, we have an opening in sports. Do you want it or not?" Kelley asked bluntly.

"Well, if you're going to put it *that* way." Patrick smiled at Kelley. "I'll take it."

"Oh." She seemed vaguely disappointed. "Okay."

"Ever written about sports?" Jason asked. "Do you play any? Hockey? Basketball? Football?"

"Does cycling count?" Patrick asked.

"Um, sure. I guess." Jason sounded a little confused. "But I don't know if we'll ever have anything to report there."

"Well, no, not until I get the team started," Patrick said. "But after that? Wow. Look out. Constant reportage."

"Yeah. Good luck with that," Jason told him under his breath.

"You can report what Jason says, after he and I discuss it," Kelley said. "Don't go off on some wild tangent."

Patrick sat back a little in his chair. "Okay then. Nothing . . . tangential." He looked at Laurie. "Is that a word?"

"It's very big in the geometry world," she told him.

While Kelley and Mr. Garcia talked with Jason about how and what to delegate, Patrick scooted his chair closer to me. "So what's this guy like?" He gestured to Mr. Garcia. "Is he cool? Does he make up for Little Miss—"

"Yes," I interrupted him. "He does."

"And there are lots of perks being on staff," Laurie said. "There's this conference in Boston and we get to go for the whole weekend—"

"So, basically, you guys are in this for a free trip to Boston." Patrick nodded.

"Well . . . *yeah*," Laurie said. "We usually go in the summer anyway, but this'll be like a bonus."

I hadn't thought yet about what it would actually mean to go there this year. Maybe I didn't really want to go back.

"Okay?" Patrick waved his hand in front of my face.

"What?" I asked.

"Boston. You, me, and 'Cause-must-kiss over here."

I nodded slowly. What was he talking about? "Sure," I said.

Laurie cleared her throat. "She just gets choked up over the idea of leaving town. And speaking of which—you know, Patrick Kirkpatrick, we're really glad you moved here. But I heard that the town's sort of miffed."

"Why's that?" Patrick asked.

"They're going to have to redo the population sign. From 902 to 905."

Patrick sort of half smiled. "Actually it's 904. Until my dad kicks me out of the house, then it'll be 903."

"And this is going to happen?" Laurie looked shocked.

Patrick shrugged. "You never know."

I looked at Patrick. So his mother wasn't around, either. I wanted to ask why, but I couldn't. That was too personal. He'd tell us eventually.

"So we have some assignments for you," Kelley said. "Did you check out some old issues?"

Patrick nodded.

"How does it look?"

"Like you need me," Patrick said. "Desperately."

"Excuse me?" Kelley glared at him. Nobody talked to Kelley like that, not really.

But I kind of thought that he was right.

CHAPTER FOUR

Salvage City was a warehouse located in an old mill building on the narrow strip of land between the canal and the
river—just like the paper factory. To drive to it, you had to
cross a narrow, one-lane bridge that was just a few feet
above the rushing water in the canal.

Living in Birch Falls made you used to bridges; you
developed an immunity or something. Whenever my grandparents or cousins visited, they seemed to be clutching
their car seats and armrests, knuckles white, bracing themselves, warding against an imminent panic attack.

You had to have the immunity because by the time
you were a senior, you were supposed to jump off the big
bridge north of the falls. You'd spray paint your initials on
the underside of the bridge, or your friends would, and
then you'd drop into the river where it pooled above the
falls. People did it in groups to be safe and also to have
witnesses so they wouldn't be accused of wimping out.

Salvage City had the following rules posted on its
entrance door:

NO WHOLESALERS.

SHOPLIFTERS WILL BE PROSECUTED.

ALL SALES ARE FINAL.

NO SMOKING.

SALVAGE CITY ASSUMES NO RESPONSIBILITY

FOR CARS LEFT OVER 24 HOURS.

But nobody paid attention to the last two rules. The far side of the Salvage City parking lot was filled with rusted-out, abandoned cars. When you went inside, the warehouse had a faint aroma of smoke, because some of the clerks chain-smoked, and some of the merchandise had been rescued from fires.

Salvage City had three types of items: brand-new, nearly new, and flat-out irregular. "Nearly new" meant that it had either fallen off or out of a truck or train or been rescued from a warehouse that had caught on fire or flooded. Natural disasters struck, and they ran to collect the stuff and sell it to us in Birch Falls—cheap. It might sound kind of strange, but I guess we all kept going to Salvage City because it was weird what got left over—what tornadoes, hurricanes, floods, and other disasters left behind.

My dad insisted on taking me and Sam there every other Sunday, which gave the store time to get new merchandise.

He was obsessed with looking for good deals, for getting the best price. "Hidden treasure," he'd call it when he found something good in the giant Overstock City section, where you could find hundreds of shirts in not quite the right color—but occasionally something semicool would show up, and Dad would say, "We'll take a flyer on this."

For my dad, going to Salvage City was as close as he got to gambling, as close as he got to taking a risk. When you found something good there, after searching through various, hopeless, unpromising bins, it was like winning the lottery. Dad and Sam would race around trying to find the best bargains and the hidden gems that everyone else had somehow missed.

Besides the remnants and closeout specials, Salvage City featured trendy clothes and used clothes. Laurie had found a cool, used leather jacket last year, and I'd bought at least four or five ten-dollar wool sweaters. It was sort of like those tables that appeared on the street in Boston, where suddenly in a rainstorm someone would be selling umbrellas for five dollars, but if it were sunny the same table would have sunglasses and hats. All really trendy stuff that you had to have but you didn't want to spend much on, so you bought knockoffs. Salvage City was full of knockoffs. It had unheard-of brands of soda, of socks, of potato sticks, of tennis balls, of shampoo.

I was holding up a pair of low-rise corduroy jeans and

contemplating whether they were last year's trend or whether they might possibly be next year's trend, when I sensed someone standing next to me.

"Hey, Alison." Patrick smiled at me.

"Hey! What are you doing here?" I asked. It sounded rude when I said it. I was just surprised to see him.

"My dad insisted we check it out. He said he's been looking out the window at it every day, and he was curious." Patrick rolled his eyes. "So I'm standing here and I'm wondering. What is the deal with this place? I mean, it's sort of retro. In a violating-every-antismoking-law-in-the-state way."

"Yeah. I know." I waved my hand in the air, and I could have sworn I saw white air move.

"So. This is the Birch Falls Mall? Or what?" Patrick asked. "Hey, they really should think about opening one. I mean—the name alone. Sweet."

"Yeah, well. Laurie and I go to Holyoke or Amherst when we want to actually buy anything," I said. "Well, if we can convince our parents to take us. If not, there's a bus."

Patrick wasn't listening to me. He was staring across the first floor at the checkout. I followed his gaze and saw a man leaning out to light the cigarette of a girl working there. I guessed he was checking out the girl—she had the kind of body that actually looked okay in a hideous, bright orange-red uniform that had definitely come from someone else's overstock of bad uniform colors.

"Oh, great," Patrick muttered. "He's hitting on a woman in a smock top."

"He is?" I asked. "Who?"

Patrick turned away from them. "This is what my dad does. He's a serial flirt."

"Serial flirt?" I repeated.

Patrick nodded. "He's horrible. He can't resist anyone with—well, you know."

Two aisles over, I saw my dad pushing a cart filled with cases of cheap soda and dented canned vegetables and fruit—his usual purchases. He hadn't hit a jackpot yet.

I felt someone tap me in the back, and turned around to see Sam standing behind me. He had jabbed me with a two-liter bottle of soda—Mister Fizzee, which almost never lived up to its name. "Patrick, this is Sam, my little brother," I said.

"Brother," Sam insisted. "Not little."

He was right. Sam was tall and lanky, and when he was wearing hockey skates he towered over me. He nearly towered over me now, anyway, in sneakers. Sam looked a lot like my dad—they were both tall, with dark brown hair and green-gray eyes.

"Okay. How about just Sam, then," I said.

"Hey, Sam," Patrick said.

Sam was carrying a couple of hockey sticks over his shoulder. I couldn't see what was wrong with them. Maybe they had gotten wet and were warped, or maybe they were just plain defective. Sam looked at Patrick. "You play?"

"No. I never learned," Patrick said. Then he laughed. "Okay, I tried to learn. But I sucked. My hand-eye coordination doesn't exist."

"Yeah?" Sam asked, smiling. "I'm on the middle school team. Plus a club team. And I'm going to this elite hockey camp this summer." He wasn't bragging, or if he was, at least he was justified. He really was an incredibly good player. He had all the athletic talent in the family.

"Impressive. I'll have to check out some games," Patrick said. "Next year, I guess."

I spotted my father watching us and moving closer with his cart. He was casting a strange look my way. "So, we'd better go," I said to Sam.

"Yeah, hang around here much longer and you'll get cancer." Patrick coughed and waved his hand in front of his face as a clerk walked past, a cigarette hanging on the edge of his lips.

I tried to smile. "Yeah."

"Besides, I've got to find my dad before he hits on that woman over there restocking the candy aisle," Patrick said. "Do they have anything good here? Any salvaged candy I'd want?"

"I don't know. We bought some shattered peanut brittle once that wasn't too bad," I told him. "So, see you Monday?" I said, before walking over to join Sam and my dad in line at the register. I glanced around for Patrick's dad but didn't see him anywhere. I looked back and saw Patrick picking up bags of no-name candy and examining them.

"Who's that?" my father asked me.

"That's Patrick," Sam said. "He's new here. He doesn't play hockey."

"Well then, what is the town doing, letting him stay." My dad shook his head. "Outrageous."

"Dad," Sam said.

"I'm calling the town council. Something needs to be done," Dad went on. "Issue that boy a hockey stick immediately. Here, let's give him one of yours." He struggled to pull a hockey stick away from Sam.

"*Dad.* Quit it," Sam said, but he was starting to laugh.

There they were, having a good time.

"Well, it's almost spring. He has nine months to pick it up," Dad said as he got out his wallet to pay for the cart of assorted salvaged loot. "*Then* we'll have a little talk with him." He looked at me. "Is he in your class?"

I nodded. "Just got here, though."

"Oh. Interesting. I wonder if his family's going to need new insurance," Dad said.

Without insurance, life was not worth living, according to Dad. He handed his business card to the curvaceous clerk behind the register, who was wearing a name tag that said, I'M NEW HERE! TREAT ME NICE! She took a drag from her cigarette and stared at his card.

"If you quit smoking, call me," Dad said. "We give discounts to nonsmokers."

• • •

We went from Salvage City to Birch Bowl. This was the second part of our Sunday routine.

"Lane twelve." Rick, the bowling alley manager—who was also the cook at the snack bar and the guy who had to chase down lost bowling balls—slid a pair of off-white shoes with green trim across the counter to me. "Size seven."

That was usually the extent of my conversations with Rick. "Size eight, actually," I told him, pushing the shoes back.

"Oh. Really." Rick stepped back and gave me a once-over, as if to determine that this was true, that I was in fact growing. I hated when adults did that. As if I were a living biology experiment. Hypothesis: girls will grow taller when given enough food. Lab results: yes.

"Why didn't Laurie come today?" Sam leaned against the counter beside me and waited for Rick to fog his size-ten shoes with disinfectant spray.

"She hates bowling," I said. "You know that." Whenever she met us here, she'd end up sitting at the snack bar, hanging out with some of the regulars, or calling her mom and asking for a ride home after twenty minutes.

"Yes, she hates bowling, but she also likes getting out of the house for any reason," Dad chimed in. "And you two *are* practically attached at the hip." He said this all of the time and therefore thought it was true.

"No, we're *not*," I said, which was what I always said in response.

As I sat down to put on my shoes, I watched Sam and Dad joking around as they selected the perfect bowling balls, even though I was pretty sure they were all the same in candlepin bowling. They did this: They joked and laughed and had fun together. Dad made a point of doing fun things with Sam. Like renting action flicks and going to high school football games and to the Basketball Hall of Fame in Springfield.

Sam was a great athlete, but he didn't have the mindset for bowling. He was too hyper. If he got a strike or spare, he'd try to do too much on his next frame and end up following it up with a gutter ball. He could get four frames of two in a row, and then get four strikes, and then strictly gutter balls to end the game.

Sam used to spend hours every day in front of the TV; he'd watch any sport available. Basketball, golf, tennis, NASCAR, baseball, pool, diving, the national cheer championships. My dad would toss books and magazines into Sam's lap while he sat in front of the TV to try to get him to read instead. He'd run circles around Sam's chair. He was very goofy about it. He posted signs on the TV that said, IF YOU HAVE SEEN SAM KEANEY, PLEASE CALL 1-800-FIND-SAM. THANK YOU. Or he'd run out in front of the TV and say it, pronouncing "Thank you very much" as if he were Elvis Presley.

Eventually Dad just got rid of cable TV. Sam switched obsessions and now he was into doing all sports instead of watching them. So he was gone from home a lot, but ironically Dad could spend more time with him now because he had to drive him to the gym, to the field, to the rec center. So I guess Dad got what he wanted, which was Sam out of the recliner, but we didn't have cable, which wasn't what I wanted.

Over the winter, they had rented snowmobiles a few times, and they'd tried to convince me to come along, but I hadn't. They'd come home with glowing faces, frostbit-looking noses, hat hair, and red ears. "We had a great time," they'd say. "You should've come with us."

And when they said that, I wanted to. I wished I could have. But I couldn't.

We were halfway through our second game, and I was standing there, holding my second ball and waiting for the machine to clear the eight fallen pins, when I heard this high-pitched laugh. Then I heard someone else laugh—it sounded like my dad. I glanced over my shoulder and saw him talking and laughing with a woman who looked vaguely familiar, and the man standing beside her.

What was he doing? I stood there and stared. He was *laughing*. How could he laugh so much in one afternoon? He never laughed at home. He sat there and stared at the walls or dozed off in a chair while trying to read. The only time he perked up at all was when Sam was around.

But whenever we were out in public, he mingled with

people. He made it look so casual, so easy. As if everyone wasn't staring at us and wondering, how are they doing? Are they all right?

Or maybe they weren't wondering, maybe they'd completely forgotten already, and I wasn't sure which was worse.

"Come on, Al. Bowl already," Sam said.

But I just stood there staring at Dad as he walked back over to our scoring table. I was so mad, I couldn't take my eyes off him.

"Are you having *fun*?" I said. I tried to keep it light, but my voice came out sounding mean and bitter.

"What's that, Alison?" Dad looked up at me.

Are you having fun? Are you enjoying yourself? Is this a *party* for you? I thought. "Nothing," I said.

"No, what?" Dad asked.

"Never mind," I said.

"Alison. Come on. What did you say?"

"*Bowl* already," Sam said again.

I turned back to the lane to take my turn. It wasn't worth it, anyway.

"Come on, Alison," Dad said. "Pick 'em up!" he called as I aimed for the two remaining pins. I reached back with my arm and concentrated, but when the ball rolled off my fingertips, it veered into the gutter.

"Gutter ball!" Sam yelled happily. That meant he still had a chance at beating me. "Too bad, Al."

Dad looked at me as I walked past the scoring table and sat in a chair as far away from him as I could. "You'll get him next game," he said in an encouraging tone. "Don't worry."

"I don't care," I said.

"Come on, Alison," Dad said. "Cheer up."

Cheer up? Who did he think he was talking to? Sometimes he seemed to be in a completely different world, as if having him say "have a nice day" and "cheer up" would just automatically make that happen, make horrible things disappear. He sounded like a bad, cheap greeting card. Maybe that worked with Sam, but not me.

"You know what?" Sam commented as I sat beside him at the scoring table a few minutes later. "You know what we should do?"

"Leave?" I mumbled.

"No." Sam elbowed me in the ribs. "We should join a bowling league. That way we'd bowl more often and we'd get really good. That could be sort of cool."

"A league? All right. Let's talk about it," Dad said, standing in front of us. "Seems to me that the first thing we have to decide is what to put on the back of our shirts. We need to ask someone to sponsor us. Right?"

"*No,*" I said.

"Come on, Al. It'll be great," Sam said. "We'll buy our own bowling balls—"

"No thanks," I said.

"And our own shoes, so we won't have to rent shoes anymore, and you won't have to talk to Rick—"

"No!" I said, not looking at either one of them. "You guys can do it, but I'm not doing it."

"You know what? You are so not fun sometimes. *So* not fun." Sam shoved out of the chair and walked up to start another game.

I knew that Sam hated me when I acted like that. I hated that about myself, after the fact, when I saw how upset he got.

"Alison, it's all right," Dad said. "We don't have to do anything you don't want to."

I just stared at the floor. Weren't we already?

CHAPTER FIVE

"Can somebody explain why we just saw a *video* in phys. ed.?" Patrick asked as we met in the *Bugle* classroom on Thursday to work on our latest articles. Laurie insisted on writing her first drafts on an old-fashioned manual typewriter at home, which meant she had to retype them into the computer at school.

"What kind of video? And was it any good?" Laurie asked, sitting down in front of a computer that had a neon green "Genius in Residence" bumper sticker on it.

"Actually, it wasn't bad. All about the Olympics," Patrick said. "But like . . . what is the teacher for?"

"You have a lot to learn about this place. 'Watch the video' are the three most-often used words in this school," Laurie said as she typed. "Whenever a teacher's at a loss for words or hasn't prepared enough material or doesn't know anything or just feels under the weather? We get videos."

"Great." Patrick sat down at a computer next to hers, while I sat at the table and got out my biology assignment to work on.

"The only one who *doesn't* show videos? Except for a Mark Twain thing once? Mr. Garcia," Laurie told him.

"I wish Mr. Lewis would show us a video," Patrick said.

"Something about how we'll never need to know geometry in real life?" I said.

"Yeah." Patrick looked over his shoulder at me and grinned. "Hey, don't you have to write something? Get over here and suffer with the rest of us."

I shrugged. "There's no news this week."

"Yeah. It *felt* like that," he said.

Laurie and I laughed. "Actually, I already finished. It was like two paragraphs about changes in the school website."

"Hard-hitting, no doubt." Patrick stared at the blank screen in front of him, then typed a few sentences, then paused. "Hey, what's that?" He reached into a bookcase beside him. "Ooh, the *High Bugle* yearbook."

Laurie laughed. "It's not the *High Bugle* yearbook."

Patrick cracked open the book. "This is last year. Let's see if you guys are in here. Let's see what your lives consisted of before sophomore year."

"Not much." Laurie looked over at me and smiled.

"State of endless boredom, wasn't it?" I added.

Patrick leaned back in his chair and flipped through the pages, while Laurie typed and I went back to my homework. I didn't pay much attention to him until he turned around and dropped the open yearbook onto the table in front of me.

"Were you a cheerleader or something in a prior life?"

"What? No," I said.

"Oh. Well, you just sort of look like one there." Patrick pointed to a large black-and-white photo. I leaned forward and looked at it.

Ryan was dressed in his football uniform shirt, and he was carrying me in his arms, holding me by the waist, as if he were about to toss me into the air. I was wearing a school T-shirt and a skirt and my hair was still long then, and it was tied up with a big ribbon, and I was smiling. And I stared at the photo, trying to remember what day that was, why Ryan was wearing his uniform shirt, why we looked so happy. I couldn't remember feeling like that. As if I didn't have a care in the world.

Laurie had wheeled over in her chair to check out the photo, too. "It's the extreme ponytail. I made her do it," she said. "It was like school spirit day or something dumb like that. We faked it, naturally."

Patrick looked at me for a second and then slammed the yearbook shut. "So much for memory lane, right?"

"So what are you writing again?" Laurie asked him as they went back to their computers and I stared at the year-book, wanting to open it and see what else I'd forgotten.

"It's the results of the track meet yesterday," Patrick said.

"Where are your notes?" Laurie asked.

"I lost them." Patrick shrugged. "It's okay, though. I remember the important stuff."

"Like what?"

"Like . . . I don't know. But I'll make it up."

"But that wouldn't be reporting," Laurie said.

Patrick turned to us and rolled his eyes. "My article is like a hundred words. I can write at least fifty about the race conditions." He turned back to the computer and started typing, reading out loud as he did: "Spring came early to Birch Falls Regional High, and records were broken as the midday sun baked the track to a fast surface."

We all started laughing.

"That's horrible," Laurie said. "That's really, really horrible."

"Thank you." Patrick grinned and leaned back in his chair.

Laurie stared at his hair for a second, then reached up and touched it, lightly bouncing against the spikes with her hand held flat. "That is some sharp hair."

"Thank you," Patrick said.

"That is like . . . porcupinesque."

As we sat there, I noticed how Laurie kept looking at him, at the way she was still gazing at his hair five minutes later, as if she wanted to touch it again.

"Is there a late bus or something?" Patrick asked when we walked out of school an hour later.

"Yeah, but not until five-thirty," Laurie said. "We'll walk."

"Is it safe here for you guys to walk home by yourselves?" Patrick asked as he stopped at the bike rack.

"Safe?" I repeated as he unlocked his bike. What did he think would happen to us?

"You obviously are still too new here. It's very safe. Tremendously safe. Ridiculously safe. Mind-numbingly, boringly safe," Laurie said.

"I'll take Adverbs for 'Safe' for four hundred dollars, Alex," Patrick said as he started riding his bike slowly beside us.

"Oh, my god. Don't tell me you like *Jeopardy*. That's my grandparents' favorite show," Laurie said.

"My mom—she's really into it. She was actually on the show once," Patrick said. "Back when she was in college. She won like ten thousand dollars."

"That is so cool," Laurie said in an admiring tone.

"Not really." Patrick rode in a small circle beside us. "Not all early *Jeopardy* winners age well. I mean, those early successes in life can turn you into a not-so-nice person."

"Not-so-nice, huh?" Laurie said. "That's pretty vague. Is that the best you can do?"

"For now. Give me a minute, though," Patrick said.

There was an awkward pause.

"So. Nice bike," I said, to change the topic.

"Thanks. This is actually my level D bike."

"D?" I asked.

"As in A, B, C, D," he said.

"You have more than one bike?" I asked.

"I have five. I race," he explained. "This is one of my old training bikes."

"Training wheels. I think I had those," Laurie joked.

"You guys ever ride?" Patrick asked.

My bike was an old ten-speed of my father's, and Laurie had a three-speed she'd bought at the Girards' yard sale two years ago for ten dollars. "Um . . . not really," I said.

"You should try it. Are you into sports?"

"Well, we both got cut from the soccer team in the fall. Does that count?" Laurie laughed. "Too bad there's no cycling team. You'd be like the king."

"Are you really going to start one?" I asked.

"I doubt it. I mean, that sounds like a lot of work. If I find someone else to ride with, cool. But I kind of like being on my own, too."

"So why'd you say you were going to?" Laurie asked.

"I don't know. Just seemed like the thing to say at the time. Like it might bother Kelley."

"Okay. Well, where are you going to race and stuff? We'd come watch," Laurie said.

"Who knows? I can barely find my way home at this point. Hey, you want to see the place?" Patrick asked. "If I can find it?"

I looked up at the big, white two-story house. Carefully pruned bushes lined the walk and the steps up to the front porch. Off behind the house was a large, gray barn and a separate two-car garage. Patrick rode his bike over to the garage, then came over to unlock the front door. We followed him inside.

"So, here's the tour. This is the house." We swiftly walked through the living room and down the hall toward the kitchen.

"Nice," Laurie commented.

"Big," I said.

"Dad hired a decorator or something, which is the only reason everything matches." Patrick opened the refrigerator. "This okay?" He handed me a can of cold root beer. "Kuzmustkiss?"

"Thanks." I looked at the bare fridge door, without a magnet or note in sight. His father's business card was taped near the handle.

"Don't worry, you're safe, because the serial flirt is not around," Patrick said as he cracked open a can of Dr Pepper. "He heard there were some waitresses over in Northampton that he hadn't hit on yet, so, you know. He had to go."

"Really." I laughed.

"No, he's still at work." Patrick sipped his soda.

"You've got mail." Laurie pointed to the answering machine on the counter. Its red message light was flashing.

"Probably Kelley wondering if I went off on a tangent." He walked over to press Play.

A few seconds later, a deep voice spoke. "Patrick. I'll be

at the office until six tonight. Remember what we talked about. When I get home, I expect you to have finished all of your homework—I really want to make sure you get off to a good start here. There are no excuses. Don't go off on some marathon bike ride, just get your work done—"

Patrick reached over and hit a button. "Messages erased," the machine said. Patrick didn't look at us for a second.

"Hey, at least your dad cares," Laurie said.

"Not really. He just doesn't want me to flunk out. Any bad grades and he'll ground me. Or ship me off somewhere else."

"He wouldn't," I said. "How could he?"

Patrick set down his empty soda can and it clattered against the tile counter. "You don't know my dad."

"Yeah, well, I also don't know *my* dad, so there's that." Laurie quickly explained how her father had left them, how he'd had an affair and then gone off and started a second family before he and Mrs. K. even finalized their divorce. She hated him for it, and I hated him by extension. Laurie usually tore up his letters and threw out birthday presents from him—not that they came all that often.

Patrick turned to me. "So. What's your dad like?"

"He's . . . he's okay," I said. "We're actually not that close."

"Yeah, you are," Laurie said.

"No, we're not," I argued.

"Okay." She sighed. "Just in comparison, I guess."

● ● ●

By the time I got home, my father was back from work. He was standing over the stove, stirring a pot of spaghetti sauce and waiting for the water in another pot to boil. "Hey there," he said when I walked in. "How was school?"

"Okay." I shrugged. "You know." I dropped my bag onto an old chair underneath the wall phone.

"Okay?"

"Yeah."

"Well, that's good." He held up a spoonful of spaghetti sauce for me to taste, but I shook my head. "Anything else?"

"We stayed afterward to study for a while."

"You and Laurie?"

I nodded. Then I went upstairs to my bedroom, before he could ask any more about my day.

If I had a decorating theme, it would have to be "less is more." My room had two windows with blue-flowered curtains and a bed with a matching quilt. I didn't have much on the walls, which were painted white. I had a few pictures stuck to my oversized black bulletin board (a Salvage City "jackpot," actually, and it wasn't even warped), which had a big open spot in the middle, covered in fluorescent-colored pushpins that used to hold other photos.

I didn't keep much on top of my dresser—a few bottles of moisturizer and perfume, and a small purple lamp. "You're not neat, you're fanatical," Laurie said about the way I kept my clothes folded and neatly stacked in my dresser and hung according to season in my closet. It wasn't as if I had that many. They weren't difficult to organize.

I went over to the bulletin board and saw that the picture of me and Ryan from the yearbook, the one Patrick had found, was still up there. I stared at it, for a second remembering how it felt when he'd whisked me up in his arms like that and twirled me around. Ryan could be sweet, a little too sweet sometimes.

I looked at myself in the small oval mirror over my dresser. How had I looked like that photo? That girl didn't look like me at all.

I reached over and pulled out the pink pushpin. I removed the photo and stuck the pushpin back into the middle of the bulletin board. Then I reached onto the top shelf in my closet and pulled out a shoebox—size seven, from last year.

I lifted the lid and dropped the photo on top of the stack inside, then I put the lid back on and pushed the box to the back of the closet shelf.

CHAPTER SIX

"Why are you sitting here?" I asked.

"Because," Ryan said. "What's your problem?"

Laurie and I were eating lunch in the cafeteria on Friday, and Ryan had just pulled up a chair at the head of the oblong table and slid into it.

"There's no problem," I said.

"Except this food," Laurie said. We were served fish sticks every Friday, no matter how often Laurie wrote a column condemning the tradition.

Kevin and Paul squeezed into seats across from us. Maybe Laurie and I were attached at the hip, like my father always teased us—but if we were, then Ryan, Kevin, and Paul were, too. Kevin picked up a fish stick, covered it with salt, and ate it in one bite. He had about a dozen on his plate. I could barely stomach one. I kept dipping a potato chip in tartar sauce, not eating it, and then dipping it again. Fish Stick Friday was always a challenge. Having Ryan sit so close wasn't making it any easier. I thought maybe I'd feel something for him. I almost wanted to. But I didn't. It was like we'd never even been together.

"Alison?" Ryan said, waving a fish stick in front of my eyes. "How's it going?"

"Good," I said, nodding, "except for that smell." I waved his hand away from my face.

"Sorry," Ryan said. "It's going okay, though?"

I shrugged. "Sure. Whatever you say."

He gave me this cute little half smile. "What are you doing this weekend?"

What are *you* doing, I wanted to say. Why are you sitting here and being nice to me and flirting with me?

"Wait, don't tell me. You're shopping and then painting your nails," Paul said.

Laurie held up her polish-free hand in front of him. "Yeah. *That* sounds like us, McGowan."

"Looks like you could use a makeover," Kevin said.

"Shut up," Laurie said. "Your personality could use a makeover."

"Ooh, Kuzmuskus. I love it when you talk tough," Kevin said as he salted another fish stick. He held it in front of Laurie's face for a second before eating it in one bite.

"Actually? We have big plans for the weekend," Laurie said, backing up a little from him. "Big. Huge."

"Yeah, right," Paul said. "We believe that."

"I'm serious!" Laurie said. "We're going to Boston. Right, Alison?"

"R—right." I raised my eyebrows and looked at her. What was she up to?

"Cool," Paul said.

"Yeah. Maybe we'll come with you," Kevin said.

"In your dreams," Laurie told him.

"So are you leaving tonight? You won't be down at the launch?" Ryan gave me a searching look.

I started thinking that he had too much time on his hands, now that he was out of sports to do. Hockey season was over, and his status around school was sort of slipping, so he wanted to get me back. Probably just to prove that he could, that Ryan Bouchard didn't get dumped.

Suddenly Patrick came up to the table and stopped right beside my seat. "Hey, we still hanging out tomorrow— you guys still coming over?"

The guys all looked up at Patrick and then down at me. Ryan wasn't giving me the soulful puppy look anymore. He was glaring at me, the way he had when I stopped talking to him for a few weeks.

"So you're not going to Boston. Then why did you say that, Kuzmuskus?" Kevin asked.

"Because you were giving us a hard time. Because why do we owe you an explanation for anything?"

Ryan frowned at her, then turned back to Patrick. "Who *are* you, anyway?" he asked.

"Nice introduction, Bouchard. This is Patrick Kirkpatrick," Laurie said. "Patrick, this is Ryan, Kevin, and Paul. Don't mind them. They think they own this place."

"I'm Patrick Kirk," Patrick said. "Hey."

"Patrick's from Maine," Laurie added.

"Oh, yeah? So, you play hockey?" Ryan asked.

Patrick shook his head.

"Who comes from Maine and doesn't play hockey?" Paul said, as if Patrick had committed a mortal sin.

"About a hundred thousand people," Patrick said. "Give or take a hundred thousand." He just stood there, arms crossed in front of him, his yellow messenger bag across his shoulder.

"Football then," Ryan said. "You play football?"

It was like they were in a foreign country and they were desperately trying to find out if he spoke the same language.

Patrick shook his head. "Nope. I try to avoid things with teams."

"Whatever." Kevin salted yet another fish stick and muttered, "Freak." Which was funny, coming from him. Who was the bigger freak—someone who raced on a bicycle or someone who needed his own salt lick?

I felt like I should come to Patrick's defense. I couldn't stand the way those guys were talking to him. "Patrick's a cyclist. And he's really good," I said.

"He's a what?" Paul said.

"A cyclist," Laurie said. "You know, like Lance Armstrong." I could tell she was enjoying telling the know-it-all something he didn't know.

"But without the winning the Tour-de-France-multiple-times part," Patrick added.

"Yeah, well, and skip the cancer part while you're at it," Laurie said.

Patrick laughed, and his eyes were sort of sparkling when he looked at me. He pulled a chair over from the next table and sat down next to me. I could see Ryan glaring at him, obviously annoyed he'd interrupted our lunch.

"Come on, guys," Ryan said. "Let's go outside."

"Aren't we entertaining you enough?" Laurie asked.

"Fish Stick Friday sucks," Patrick said as he dipped his pinky finger into the tartar sauce on my plate.

"You're just realizing this *now*?" Laurie asked.

Ryan put his hand on the back of my chair before he walked away. "If you're around this weekend, call me. Or just come to the launch tonight. Okay?" he said in a soft voice.

"Sure," I said, and I saw that his hand was on my shoulder, rubbing it. I knew he was trying to flirt with me by giving me this mini-backrub, but I didn't feel anything. I didn't understand why he wanted me to call him. How could he still be expecting that?

"I'm serious, Alison," he said. "Okay?"

I nodded. "Sure."

When he left, Patrick reached over to take some potato chips off my plate. "Alison, it's okay if *he's* serious. Just as long as you're not. Okay?" I laughed. "No, really. Promise me." He pushed a paper napkin toward me and pulled a pen out of his bag. "Put it in writing."

"You're not serious," I said. "Because you know I'm

not going to call him."

"Are you sure?" Patrick asked. "Because you said, 'sure,' which might mean that you're going to."

"Don't worry about Alison," Laurie said. "She already went out with him. It didn't work out."

"You and him? Really?" Patrick stared at me. "Wait a second. That's the guy from the yearbook picture. You led his cheers!"

"No, I didn't," I said. I felt my face start to turn red.

Laurie crunched a potato chip. "Anyway, don't worry—they're not getting back together. Alison's finished with Ryan. She never dates anybody. That's one of the Alison rules."

"It's a rule? Not to date anybody?" Patrick looked at me. "Um . . . I hate to quote someone else, but . . . 'cause why?"

"No, it's not a rule. It's just . . . "

"You know the expression 'hard to get'? Well, she's impossible to get."

"Shut up. I am not," I said. "And there aren't any rules about it."

"Ahem. You are, and there are," Laurie said.

I shook my head, dismissing Laurie's comments. "Look, can we change the subject? I mean, what are we doing this weekend? Seriously. We need a plan." Or at least, I needed a plan, to get me out of the house.

"Here's the plan. We're hitching a ride to Boston. We're taking the bus. We're cashing in our vast trust funds and renting a limo," Laurie said.

Patrick just raised his eyebrows and stared at her.

Laurie sighed. "We *could* go to the launch, I guess. It's sort of the place people go on weekend nights and you haven't been there yet."

"Well, now I *have* to check it out," Patrick said.

"Yeah, but do we really want to go, if they're going to be there?" I said.

"The launch," Patrick said. "What's that? You have rocket competitions? The space shuttle takes off there?"

"The *boat* launch," I corrected him. "By the river. Halfway between the two bridges."

"And it's the place to be? Why?"

I shrugged. "It just is."

"Okay. So do I bring a boat?" Patrick asked.

"We usually do. The cabin cruiser. The catamaran," Laurie said. "Whatever's handy."

Patrick smiled. "Right."

We headed out on our bikes from Laurie's house at eight o'clock. Unfortunately it was already dark out and hard to see where we were going, unless a car passed us and its headlights shone for a few seconds on the road in front of us.

"This thing is supposed to have three gears, right? So how come nothing happens when I press this lever? It is completely shot," Laurie complained.

"How about this? This has to be the loudest bike in

history," I said as I changed gears and there was a loud "clank," as if I'd broken something.

It had taken me half an hour to clean up my dad's old ten-speed after I got it out of the garage. Cobwebs were clinging to the spokes, and there was dust all over the seat and handlebars. I hosed it down and used a bucket of soap and water and a sponge to clean it so that it didn't look totally disgusting. Then I filled up the tires with some air and oiled the chain, just like my dad had insisted I learn to do when he gave me the bike. I was just about to go inside and leave a note when Dad and Sam pulled into the driveway in the Subaru wagon.

"Hey!" Dad waved as he got out of the car. "Where are you going on that bike?"

"Just out," I said.

"Oh, yeah? We're going to a movie tonight," Sam said. "Want to go?"

I pictured them watching a comedy, laughing, munching on popcorn, Sam tossing it at me if I went along. "No thanks, " I said. "I already made plans."

"Where . . . what?" Dad asked, sounding a little befuddled.

"Laurie."

"Oh. Friday night, of course. Okay."

"Have fun at the movie," I said to Sam as I rode past him.

He just glared at me. "Yeah. Whatever."

"Last one to the bottom is a rotten fish!" Laurie now called over her shoulder as we went faster and faster down the steep hill toward the river. She was in front of me, and her long brown hair streamed out behind her, whipping in the wind. It was just like when we were little kids and we rode our bikes all over the place—how we'd get going as fast as we could and then let go of the handlebars.

My hair used to be long then, too—we competed to see who could grow it the longest. For some reason I'd cut mine short when Mrs. K. took us to her beauty salon for a treat last November and tried to convince us to change, to try something new. Laurie was smart and resisted. I was still trying to grow mine out.

We were both flying when we got to the bottom of the hill and had to turn right onto Miller Road. All of a sudden I saw a bike coming from the other direction, fast. I swerved out of the way, and Laurie shrieked and slammed on her brakes.

Patrick nearly crashed right into her, but he made a last-second swerve to get around her.

He circled and came back to us. "Man! You guys ever hear of bike lights?"

"Hey, we had the right of way," Laurie said, out of breath.

"Hardly." Patrick shook his head, then his mouth broke into a wide smile. "Hey, Alison. Miss Kuzmustkiss."

"Patrick Kirkpatrick," Laurie replied.

"Can't say much for your bike-riding skills," Patrick said.

"It's not me, it's this bike," Laurie said. "The brakes don't work, it's impossible to maneuver, and instead of having three gears like it's supposed to, it only has one."

"That bike's a classic, though." Patrick moved a little closer to her to check out the maroon three-speed bike with a bike rack on the back and a round bell on the handlebars. "Where'd you get it?"

"Yard sale. And let me just say that it is true—you get what you pay for. Ten dollars equals one gear. Ratio of cash to gears is ten to one."

"Wow. You *are* good at math," Patrick said.

"Shut up." Laurie laughed and pushed off with one foot. "Come on, let's go."

The three of us rode side by side in the breakdown lane, which wasn't really wide enough for that. After a few near crashes, when we tried to scoot over as a car passed, Patrick said, "You guys would be horrible in the peloton."

"The pela-what?" I asked.

Laurie glanced over at me. "Did he just insult us?"

"The peloton. You know, in bike races there's this pack of riders—sometimes behind the leaders, sometimes it includes the top riders. And they all stick really close together—it's part of race strategy."

"Okay," Laurie said slowly. "So what does that have to do with us?"

"So, you can't be weaving around in the peloton or everyone would crash," Patrick explained.

"I'll have to remember that. Next time I'm in the tour de whatever," Laurie said. "But in the meantime, let's try to remember that this bike is old, slow, and two sizes too big for me, *Lance*."

Patrick laughed as we turned down the road to the boat launch. "Okay, fine. Hey, Alison, I can fix that noise for you—bring your bike over to my house sometime."

There were five cars and two pickup trucks parked at the launch. I recognized Ryan's pickup right away. I remembered the time Laurie and I rode in the back together, the first time Ryan asked me out, flying down the road, screaming as we went over a bump on the way to the I-C Treat. That seemed like ten years ago, instead of one.

We stood in the parking lot for a minute. There wasn't a bonfire tonight, but I could hear voices over by the river—some guys and some girls, too.

"So. This is it?" Patrick looked around. "Where is everyone?"

"Follow me," Laurie said. She took off on her bike, her tires crunching along the dirt and gravel footpath to the river.

Patrick went after her, and I followed him.

A bunch of guys were sitting on washed-up logs and rocks at the top of the boat ramp.

I came to a stop a few feet away from Ryan. My bike

skidded in the sandy dirt when I stopped, and I nearly tipped over.

"Careful." Ryan smiled when he looked at me. But when he looked over at Patrick, his expression changed. "You guys out for a little bike ride?" He made it sound as if we were stupid, as if this were an idiotic thing to do on a Friday night.

"Yes," I said.

"Hey, Alison," Kevin said. "We were just thinking of going out in the rowboat. Want to come?"

"You're really good at rowing, aren't you, Kuzmuskus?" Paul said.

"You know that oarlock's broken, right?" I said.

"That'll just make it more fun," Ryan said. "So, what's he doing here?" He gestured toward Patrick. "What are you, their mascot or something?"

"Oh, yes. Exactly. You're brilliant. You guessed it right away," Patrick told him.

Ryan narrowed his eyes. "You know, we invited Alison and Kuzmuskus down here. Not you."

"Hey—I have a great idea. Who wants to go river biking?" Laurie asked.

"Um . . . not me," I said.

"I can't get this bike wet," Patrick said. "Are you crazy?"

"Chickens," Laurie said. "You're both such chickens!" She charged down the ramp toward the water. Kevin sprinted after her, shouting at her, and we all laughed as she rode right into the river, up to pedal height, then wobbled slightly and tipped over. She hopped off the bike and ended up standing knee-deep in water on the concrete ramp.

"Nice!" Ryan called to her, as Kevin grabbed the bike. He pulled it out of the river, and he and Laurie walked back toward the rest of us. Laurie's jeans were wet up to the knees, and the sleeves of her red long-sleeved "SuperStar" T-shirt were sopping.

"Way to go, superstar," Paul said.

"Well, it's a concept that needs work." Laurie shivered and rubbed her arms. "That water is freezing tonight." She took her bike back from Kevin.

"I bet that thing rusts through in ten minutes," Paul said, laughing. "All the pieces are going to fall off."

"So we'll ride home fast. No offense, but this place is dead anyway." Laurie swung her leg over the bike and took off, and Patrick followed her, calling "See ya!" over his shoulder.

Before I could move, Ryan reached out to grab my bike. "Let me go," I said as he gripped my back wheel, and my front wheel churned to a stop in the sandy dirt. "Come on. Let me go." The red flashing safety light on the back of Patrick's bike was vanishing up the path.

"Why? You don't have to leave, just because they are," Ryan said. "Hang out for a while."

"I can't. I have to get home," I said.

"It's only eight forty-five."

"Yeah, but by the time I get there—"

He grabbed the hood of my sweatshirt, then moved his hand down to the middle of my back. "I'll give you a ride. We can put your bike in the back of my truck. Remember?"

"Alison!" Laurie's voice rang out. "Come *on*!"

"Coming!" I called back to her. "So I'll see you at school," I told Ryan, trying to get him to let go of me. "Okay?"

"Yeah. Okay, Alison. Sure." He let go and gave me a violent push forward.

Patrick was waiting for me in the parking lot. "Everything okay?"

"Sure." I just rode past him. I didn't want to talk about it.

"So what was going on back there? When you were with Ryan?" Laurie asked as we pedaled toward her house, her bike still trailing drops of water and mine screeching every time I changed gears. We'd split up with Patrick at the top of the hill. "What happened?"

"Nothing happened," I said.

"He tried to kiss you again, didn't he?"

I shook my head. "No, he was holding on to my bike. He wanted me to stay."

"He is so not over you."

"I don't know. Maybe," I said.

We coasted into Laurie's driveway, and I leaned my bike against the garage. Mrs. K.'s car was parked outside it, as usual, because the garage was full of old clothes, exercise equipment, and other things she was saving for her next major yard sale. She drove a used royal-blue Plymouth Sundance, which she had bought because she liked the name. "Yeah, Sundance. It's a good name . . . for a *stripper*, Mom," Laurie had told her.

"You know what? I'd kill to have someone that obsessed with me," Laurie said.

"He's not obsessed."

"No, but he isn't going out with anyone else, is he? And Ryan. He pretty much always had a girlfriend, didn't he? Before you, I mean?" Laurie asked. "You know what it is? It's that whole hard-to-get thing you play with him. That makes him totally crazy."

"It's not like . . . a game to me," I said. "I'm not *playing* hard to get."

"I know. You're not playing at all," Laurie said as she opened the back door to the house. She said it in an accusing tone, as if I was doing something wrong.

"What does that mean?"

"Nothing. Forget it." The screen door slammed shut behind her.

CHAPTER SEVEN

"Ryan called you last night," my dad said when I got home the next morning. I went into the kitchen to get a glass of water, and he followed me down the hall. It was almost like he'd been waiting for me to show up. "He called pretty late, actually. I think it was after eleven."

"Really?" I couldn't believe it. I remembered how it felt when he was holding on to my sweatshirt, how he wasn't giving up on me anymore, how he wouldn't leave me alone.

"So I haven't heard about Ryan in a while."

"Mm," I said.

"Why is that?"

He sounded just like Kook. How was I supposed to talk to my dad about this? "We're not really . . . going out. Anymore." I opened the kitchen cabinet and got out a glass.

"Oh," my father said. "Really?" He watched me for a minute, as I turned on the tap and filled the glass with water. It was like he was expecting me to open up and tell him all about what had happened with Ryan when there was nothing to tell. "Well, okay. So, what are your plans today? What are you and Laurie going to do?"

"I don't know yet," I said.

"Hm. Well, Sam and I will be away at his baseball game for most of the day. But I was thinking." He hesitated, looking a little nervous. "I want us all to go out for pizza at Jerry's tonight. How does that sound?"

"Okay," I said, even though it didn't sound okay, even though it was the last place in town I wanted to go. But if I tried to tell him that, we'd end up in a big, awkward discussion. Or no discussion at all. And which was worse? They both made me feel sick inside.

I didn't understand why everyone else wanted to go back to places, why they wanted to stare at old scenes, old photos, why they wanted to put up even more—they dug through old negatives and made new prints—when it was like asking to stand on the tracks and be hit by a train. Over and over again. Why do that? I didn't shove things in my face just to see how bad it felt. Not like Sam, who would take out old birthday cards and stare at them until his eyes got red and then run upstairs and slam his door and turn on loud music. Not like Dad, staying up late, leafing through cards and letters from friends, until he collapsed on the couch and I'd see him there in the morning, curled up, his face pale gray, under a fleece throw or his blue canvas jacket. And I'd be afraid to wake him up and tell him it was time for work, because sometimes when I first woke up I'd be happy, because I didn't remember what had happened for the first few seconds. I didn't want to take that away from him.

"So we'll meet back here around . . . say, six," Dad said. "Six o'clock. Okay?" He patted my shoulder awkwardly.

"Can I bring Laurie?" I asked.

"Don't see why not. I'll call Jody and invite the two of them, okay?" Then he left the kitchen and I heard him yell up the stairs, "Sam! We're going in ten minutes—you ready?"

I walked past him while he was still yelling and went upstairs. As I was walking past Sam's room, the loud music suddenly shut off, and he opened the door. "Hey. What are you doing home?" he asked.

"Showering. Changing," I said.

"Oh. Right." He nodded. "Did you ever notice that you treat this place like a locker room?"

"What?"

"I mean, hurry up, you wouldn't want to hang around or anything and actually live here," Sam said. Then he went back into his room and closed the door.

Jerry's Tavern was located two blocks from Riverbank Paper's main entrance.

I didn't look at the paper company, if I could avoid it. I'd hold my breath, count to ten, the way other people did when they drove past cemeteries, and we'd be past it. Of course, I couldn't avoid smelling the paper factory sometimes, but that was something I was so used to that I really didn't notice it most of the time. You got used to it, living here, the way you got used to narrow, high bridges.

So far I'd avoided Jerry's, too. It hadn't been hard, because my dad hadn't shown any interest in going—maybe because it was the Riverbank workers' hangout, not his insurance agency's place. I wondered what had made him decide this was the night of our return.

"Hey!" Jerry, the owner, greeted us warmly when we walked in. He came out from behind the bar and reached for Dad's hand to shake. "Long time no see."

"Hi there," my dad said.

Jerry looked at me and smiled. "How many tonight?"

I knew Jerry knew, and he wasn't trying to be mean. It's just that innocent questions came out that way now. *How many tonight?*

"Six," Laurie said, stepping up beside me. Sam had brought his friend Bobby, the only kid in his class who was taller than he was and who was therefore recruited to play basketball instead of hockey. For a while he actually tried being on both teams; Sam convinced him to stay on hockey because they were a good wing-center combination. Bobby was eager to please like that.

"How 'bout that round table over there?" Laurie asked Jerry.

"Sure thing, Laurie," Jerry said. "Gosh, you're getting tall—both you and Sam," he commented to me as we headed for the table.

"She's annoying that way," Laurie said. "Tall, pretty—"

"Horrible at geometry," I said.

"Oh, yeah. There is that." Laurie pulled out one of the wooden chairs and sat down at the table. "Want to trade lives?"

"Sure," I said, sitting next to her. "How about tonight?"

We all sat down and quickly decided how many pizzas we wanted and which kind. There wasn't a menu at Jerry's—just a board on the wall with your basic pizza and grinder options.

"Alison? Want to put something on the jukebox?" Laurie asked after we'd ordered.

"Um, no," I said.

"Come on," Laurie said. "Do you expect me to do everything? All you have to do is pick one song, and I'll pick the other two. And I've already got two quarters."

"No," I said again.

"Not fun. So not fun," Sam commented to Laurie.

"Well, then, I'll do it," Laurie said. "And you'll all have to suffer with my taste." She marched off to the jukebox over by the window, while Sam convinced Bobby to pay for a couple of pinball games.

As soon as they were gone, I knew I'd made a mistake. Now I was stuck with Dad and Mrs. K., the three of us sitting at that table that was clearly too big for us. They started making small talk about work. I looked around the bar at everyone, wondering if it was the same Saturday night crowd. It had been a long time since I was last here. I didn't want to think how long, but Kook's voice kept reminding me. *It's been six months, hasn't it? How are you coping?*

It had been even longer since we stopped coming to Jerry's. That had to have been last June.

"Alison," I suddenly heard my father saying. "Would you like some?" He held out a plastic cup of soda to me.

"Sure." I took it from him and glanced over at the jukebox. I hoped Laurie wouldn't pick a sad song.

"You didn't tell me you guys were going to Boston with the school paper," my father said. "What else are you hiding from me?"

"God only knows," Mrs. K. said. "Right, Charlie? I mean, they've got their little secrets. And now they're always off with that Patrick Kirkpatrick—"

Laurie slid into her chair. "Mom, that's not his name. Only I'm allowed to call him that."

"See? See what I mean. *Secrets.*" Mrs. K. smiled. "Why don't I hear music?"

Laurie rolled two quarters across the table to her mom. "The jukebox is busted. No juke tonight."

My father took a sip of beer and looked at us. "So who is this Patrick?"

"You met him at Salvage City a couple of weeks ago, remember?" I said.

He shook his head. "I didn't meet him. I saw you *talking*

85

to him. That's different."

"He's Patrick. He's funny. And smart—well, except for math, maybe. He moved here from Maine," I said.

"His father is running Riverbank now," Mrs. K. added.

"Ah. I see," my father said, as if that explained anything about who Patrick was.

"You know what? He's into cycling—you know, fifty- and hundred-mile rides and stuff like that." Laurie stuck a straw into her cup of soda. "Oh, my god. A hundred miles. He could probably ride all the way to Boston. Isn't that weird?"

"Yeah, but once he got there, then he'd have to take the bus home," I pointed out.

Laurie shuddered. "Yuck. The bus."

"There's nothing wrong with the bus," my father said. "It's economical, direct, and you don't have to worry about parking—"

"Obviously you've never had to sit next to a snoring middle-aged guy with bad cologne and roving hands," Laurie said to him.

"What?" Mrs. K. burst out laughing. "When was this?"

"Remember—it was like three years ago, pre-Sundance, and your other car was broken down, so we all took the bus, and we stayed overnight somewhere near downtown, and on the way back on Sunday we got to the bus station late and the bus was really crowded so we couldn't sit next to each other?" Laurie said. "Then."

"Oh." Mrs. K. looked confused. "You never told me about that guy, though."

"I was trying to *shield* you," Laurie said. "Anyway, back to the point. Would it be okay if we went over to Patrick's tonight to watch a movie?"

"I don't know. Why don't we just see how late it is when we get out of here? I think an early night sounds good," my father said.

"Why don't you girls watch movies with me tonight? Mrs. K. asked. "And you, too, Charlie. And the boys. The more the merrier, right?"

Underneath the table, Laurie nudged me with her foot. When I looked at her, she rolled her eyes. "They treat us like we're twelve. It's ridiculous."

"I know," I said.

Jerry delivered our pizzas to the table. He served slices onto paper plates and passed them around the table to all of us. Sam and Bobby sprinted over from the pinball machine and nearly leaped into their seats. It looked so good, my mouth was watering. I picked it up to take a bite, and then the smell hit me—the tomato, sausage, and green pepper— the same combination pizza that we'd eaten here a hundred times before, and I set the slice back on my plate. We shouldn't be here. We weren't supposed to be here.

CHAPTER EIGHT

A few days later we were in geometry class, working on an in-class assignment, straight out of the textbook, while Mr. Lewis graded our latest "pop" quiz.

Patrick tapped his pen against the desk like a drumstick. I hadn't seen him write anything yet. Laurie was busy measuring angles with her protractor, the way I should have been. I was staring at the question and deciding to start all over, because the first time I'd tried to do the proof, I hadn't gotten anywhere. Which sort of described how I'd done on the quiz, although I'd spat back a couple of memorized things, as requested. It just felt like there was this part of my brain that refused to pitch in when necessary.

Mr. Lewis rapped his knuckles against his desk. "Mr. Kirk. Please approach the desk."

"God, he makes it sound like a courtroom," Laurie complained in a whisper.

"Wish me luck," Patrick said under his breath as he got to his feet.

I watched as Patrick crouched beside Mr. Lewis's desk and they started talking. Mr. Lewis didn't usually call you up for C's. I should know. I was coasting on a 77 average. He definitely called you up for D's and F's.

I'd have to warn Patrick that if he didn't bring up his grades, he'd be summoned to Kook's office.

Up front, Mr. Lewis and Patrick spoke in low voices for a while, until I heard Patrick say, "But I *am* studying!"

They talked for a few more minutes. Then Patrick came back to his seat, clutching a stack of paper. He slid into his chair and dropped the papers onto his desk. I reached over to pick up one that fluttered onto the floor.

"So?" Laurie asked.

Patrick sighed. "So, huge news flash. I got a D on the last quiz. A D minus would be more accurate," he said in a low voice, keeping his eye on Mr. Lewis, who was grading more quizzes.

"So you'll catch up," Laurie said. "Don't worry. I can help you, you know."

"He said I have to take the quiz again." He shuffled the sheets of paper on his desk into a neat stack. The top one was covered with red-ink corrections. "He said I have to take every freaking quiz again until I get at least a C on all of them, or he's not passing me, and if I don't pass, then I'll have to take this class next year, too. Which isn't in the *plan*. To get off to a good start."

"Kirkpatrick, cheer up. You won't fail. I'll help you,"

Laurie said again. "I didn't know you were having such a hard time."

"Yeah, well, it's not something I want to advertise. How clueless I am. I understand bike geometry perfectly. But this?"

"It's the same thing," Laurie said. "It probably makes more sense when it's a bike because you can see it three-dimensionally, but—"

Mr. Lewis cleared his throat loudly and stood up. "Mr. Kirk, Ms. Kuzmuskus. That's enough talking back there. More than enough."

"Yes, sir," Laurie said.

At least we didn't have to worry about the usual threat, of being separated in class, because Mr. Lewis couldn't separate anyone. It would mess up the seating plan.

"We're just arranging a tutoring schedule," Laurie added. "All right, Mr. Lewis?"

"Well, that sounds like a good idea." He nodded. "A very good idea. Let me know the details once you've worked it out."

A few minutes later, when we were all still trying to complete the in-class assignment—well, all except Laurie, who had finished and was now writing her next "Kuz Why?" column—Patrick leaned down onto his desk with a sort of flop. He put his head on his arms and turned to the side, looking at me.

I glanced over at him. The corners of his mouth were

turned up in a half smile. His hazel eyes looked more green than blue today. I wondered what made them change colors—were they like a mood ring? "You know what?" he whispered, still staring at me. "This sucks. This really, really sucks."

"Yeah. I know," I whispered back.

Suddenly Mr. Lewis was right behind us. I hadn't even noticed him leave his desk. "Mr. Kirk. Are you having trouble? Are you feeling ill?"

Patrick sat up quickly. "No."

"Then I expect you to sit upright during class. To put it in geometry terms, your back should be at a ninety-degree angle to your legs." Mr. Lewis put his hand on Patrick's shoulder and waited for him to assume the correct upright position. "Like that. Is that too much to expect?"

"No. Sorry," Patrick said.

Once Mr. Lewis had returned to his desk, Patrick wrote something down on a scrap piece of paper, and held out a note to Laurie and then to me. It said, *He expects way too much of me.*

I wrote my reply on the back of a handout, which was covered with pencil scribbles, my failed attempts at equations: *They always do.*

Laurie stopped me outside journalism class that afternoon. "Hold on, I need to talk to you," she said.

"Okay. What's up?"

"I have a confession. Not that I think it'll be a shock to you," Laurie said in a soft voice as we stepped to the side of the hallway, away from the classroom door. "This is going to sound dorky and stupid and you're probably going to laugh. But I think . . . you know. I think I'm . . . I think I'm falling for him. Totally."

"Who? Mr. Garcia?" I teased. "Not again."

She slapped me on the arm. "No. Not him."

Of course she didn't have to tell me who it was. I could see it. I had seen it. But what if Patrick didn't feel the same way about her? And everything was working out really well right now, the three of us always hanging out, having fun together. I didn't want that to change.

"You're really in love?" I asked. "Are you sure it's not just that it's spring?"

Laurie looked at me and burst out laughing. "*Spring?* I'm having a reaction to *spring?* What am I, a tulip bulb? A hibernating bear? A . . . hatching chick?"

"Hey, you are way too into your biology assignment," I said. We had to write our observations of the changing season, which meant we'd spent two entire class periods walking around in forty-degree weather, in the mud, beside the stream that ran to the river, taking notes with gloves on—notes I couldn't decipher when I got home. "All I meant was that it could be the whole spring-fever thing."

"No." She stared at me.

"Well, okay," I said. "So you're crazy about Patrick. It is Patrick, right?"

"No, it's Kelley Moroney," she said, rolling her eyes. "Of course it's him."

"Well, what are you going to do? Are you going to tell him?" I asked.

"No. That would ruin everything," Laurie said. "I'm going to wait. Remember, we have to let things develop. Naturally."

"Okay, Nurse Selkirk," I said. We both started laughing, remembering our health instructor's famous "Develop-ing—It's Not Just for Film" lecture, when she pasted body parts onto a skeleton. She said "Let things develop—naturally!" so many times that we'd wanted to get it printed on T-shirts and bumper stickers to pass out at school.

"We can all be different," Laurie said, quoting another one of the nurse's favorite phrases.

"And yet the same," I chimed in, on cue.

"But what do you think?" Laurie said a little more quietly. "Do you think he even . . . You know what? Don't tell me. I don't want to know. Anyway, things are still developing." She smiled. "So my mom and I were talking last night. And don't bite my head off, but. My mom thought maybe you'd like to go to Boston this summer when school gets out—the three of us, I mean."

"I don't know," I said. I started to get a bad feeling every time I thought about going back. I wasn't ready to say that

I would go—not even for the *Bugle* trip.

"And maybe, if it's okay with Mom, we could ask Patrick to go with us, too."

I don't know why, but that bothered me. "Why would we ask him to come?"

"Because. He's fun. Think how great it would be."

"But the three of us are probably going, anyway, for the paper."

"So that's only one trip, and I bet we have to sit in a bunch of meetings. It's not like we'll be on our own and be able to go the places we want to."

"Maybe we won't all want to go to the same places," I said.

"Okay. . . . " Laurie said slowly. "Look, this is something Mom wants to do with us. For you. And you're being so obstinate about it. Why?"

"Because," I said.

"'Cause why?"

It wasn't the time for her to say that, to be cute. "Because," I said angrily. Why did I have to explain this to her? Wasn't it so obvious? "It'll remind me of stuff I don't want to think about, okay?" We joked all the time about going back to Boston, but the thing was that I didn't want to go back. The last time we'd gone, it had been the start of everything bad.

"Alison, look. You can't just avoid everything," Laurie said. "Not forever."

I didn't say anything. She didn't understand.

"Because you have to try to—to—I don't know. Make *new* memories. As corny as that sounds."

I just stared at her. "That's the stupidest thing I've ever heard."

"I'm sorry," she said. "That didn't come out right."

"Never mind. I don't want to talk about it."

"Then *think* about it. You, me, Mom—maybe Patrick, maybe not. Just for the day. Some Saturday."

I went into the classroom without her. I didn't want to think about it. I didn't want to talk about it. How could I explain? Wasn't it obvious? Why would we do something that we used to do? We couldn't. Nothing was the same and we couldn't pretend that it was.

Laurie and Patrick breezed in about five minutes after the bell. Kelley was in the middle of explaining that she wanted to publish a special section next week. "Catch up, guys," she said. "We're doing a special issue next week. A double issue, actually."

"So what you're saying is we've got issues," Patrick said as he turned one of the computer chairs around, sat down, and rested his chin on the back of it.

Kelley just stared at him.

"At least, I do," he said.

Kelley sighed loudly. "Really, you guys. Could you try to take this seriously for once? I want to make an impact with this issue. Oh, and Patrick? I need to talk to you about that track article. You got some of the results wrong. Coach Ryan called and gave me an earful."

"Sorry," Patrick said. "I could have sworn I checked everything with him first."

"You've got to be more careful," Kelley said.

"Okay, Kel. I will be. But more important, did I tell you guys I'm having a party Saturday night? You'll all come, right?" Patrick said. He looked around the room, and when his eyes met mine, he stopped and smiled. "Right?"

CHAPTER NINE

On Friday, Laurie and I met outside the cafeteria. There was that unmistakable smell in the air of baking fish products. Laurie was carrying a large orange plastic bag that I'd never seen before. "What's in the bag?" I asked. "Lunch?"

"I wish. No, it's a surprise." She stopped and surveyed the crowd. "Ah! There he is."

I followed her past the line, across the room, and toward a long, rectangular table against the wall where Patrick was sitting with Dave and Jason, from the *Bugle*.

Laurie walked up to him and said, "Happy Saint Patrick's Day, Patrick Kirkpatrick."

Patrick looked up at her, a French fry in his hand. "What are you talking about?"

"It's your day. Isn't it?" Laurie smiled. "So you get a present."

"You actually expect me to celebrate St. Patrick's Day . . . because my name is Patrick?" he asked.

"Hey, you're the one having a party tomorrow night, so you must. Anyway, it's your day. I brought you something to wear." She opened the plastic bag and pulled out a shiny green plastic hat with a golden shamrock on the front. There was an orange band around the brim.

Patrick examined the hat, then spun it around on his fingertips. "Do you seriously think that Saint Patrick wore a green plastic hat? I mean . . . plastic?"

Laurie crumpled the empty plastic bag and tossed it onto his tray. "Look, it's a theme—go with it. I'd kill to have a major holiday named after me."

"But this isn't named after *me*—" Patrick protested.

"Whatever." She pulled out a chair and sat down at the table. "You know what I mean. It's not like we all get them. Saint Laurie? I don't think so. Saint Alison? Maybe," she said.

"No way," I said as I sat down, too.

"But wait. Saint Kuzmuskus." Dave snapped his fingers. "Isn't she the patron saint of long last names?"

Patrick laughed and pulled the hat down over his hair. "So? Saintly or what?"

He looked sort of ridiculous. "You could so get away with . . . absolutely *nothing* in that hat," I said.

"That's because we need some snakes for this costume to be really effective. Saint Patrick drove the snakes out of Ireland, right?" Patrick glanced up at me from under the hat brim.

Laurie raised her eyebrow. "Snakes? If you say so."

"You know what would be close? Maybe I could drive

all the fish sticks out of the cafeteria," Patrick said. "'Cause why? 'Cause Fish Stick Friday sucks."

"Yes! Oh, my god—you have to do it," Laurie told him.

"And could you get rid of the Salisbury steaks while you're at it?" I asked. "They disgust me."

"Okay, but I'm not taking out any lunch ladies. Not even for you." Patrick smiled at me again.

"No? Not even the mean ones who skimp on fries and dole out extra lima beans?" I asked.

Laurie got to her feet. "Come on, we have bigger fish to fry," she said.

"You did not just say that." Patrick stared up at her. "And if you did, I did not just hear that. But okay, let's go. Come on." He tugged at my sleeve as he walked past. "You've got to come with, in case she makes any more bad puns."

The three of us were shoving one another and laughing as we made our way through the now-nearly-gone line, past the tower of trays and the vats of silverware. We stood on the other side of the sneeze guard, staring in at the fish shapes on display.

"That looks like an actual fish," I said, pointing to a large battered and fried piece. "Doesn't it?"

"Is that a flounder?" Patrick said. "Or is that just an extra gob of batter?"

"No, I think . . . I think it's two fish sticks . . . mating," Laurie said, and we all started laughing.

"Can I help you?" Florence, one of the lunch ladies, asked, holding tongs in her right hand and an empty plastic green plate in her left.

"Hello, this is Saint Patrick. He's here to save the world from fish sticks," Laurie said, tapping the top of Patrick's hat. "Or if not the world, then at least this town."

Florence raised her right eyebrow. "Is that so."

We were running out of the cafeteria, still laughing, when the Gods were heading in, as if they were in no hurry, as if they had two lunch periods instead of the usual one. And probably they did. They got huge breaks just for scoring multiple goals and touchdowns. That's what made them Gods.

I hadn't seen them—not to talk to, anyway—since the last launch night, when Ryan had held my bike hostage.

"Hey," Ryan said to me, grabbing my elbow as I walked past, but in a nice way this time. He was always finding these ways to hold on to me. I didn't mind, but I didn't feel anything, either.

"Hi." I shifted the shoulder strap on my bag. "How's it going?"

"Good," he said. He looked at Patrick. "Nice *hat*."

"Thank you. Thank you very much." Patrick lifted the green hat and tipped it toward the Gods. "Good day—"

Ryan suddenly grabbed the hat out of his hand. The plastic crackled as he crushed the brim. Then he tossed it over Patrick's head to Paul, who flipped it across the hall to Kevin.

"He's a *saint*, okay? You don't assault a saint," Laurie said, walking back toward us. "Or his hat. His hat is sacred."

"This isn't sacred," Kevin said as he examined the hat. "This is cheap."

"No, it's not," Laurie said. "Give it back!" She was jumping up and down, trying to get the hat out of Kevin's hands, but he tossed it to Ryan, who was even taller.

Suddenly we were all fighting for the hat—it was like a playground game from kindergarten, only rougher. Every time one of the Gods threw the hat, one of us would jump and try to intercept it, which was impossible since they were easily a foot taller than me and Laurie, but we kept trying, and the more we were trying, the harder I was laughing. Laurie was shrieking, and Patrick was clapping his hands above his head, trying to knock the hat out of the air each time it whizzed past him.

"Come on, break it up, break it up! *Now!*" a familiar voice yelled. Except that I'd never heard him speak like that before—so loudly, so angrily.

I stepped away from the Gods and toward Mr. Cucklowicz. I was breathing as hard as if I'd just run a sprint. I leaned against the wall, still laughing. The Gods stepped back, too, but they kept tossing the hat around.

"What's going on here?" Kook asked.

"Hat bashing," Laurie said. "They attacked our personal style. Literally."

"Whose hat is that?" Kook said. Even he was giving the green hat disparaging looks. I would have given anything to see Kook in that hat. And when I thought about that, I started laughing even harder. I could see him wearing the hat in his office, sitting in front of his wrestling-team felt banners and his crooked diplomas, blaring classical music; I could see him walking into the gym for practice wearing the hat with his wrestling jumpsuit; I could see how he'd look like a leprechaun.

"Ahem. It's my hat," Patrick said, as the Gods moved on to playing Frisbee with the hat. The Gods didn't listen to teachers. In some ways they had more power around school than teachers—and definitely more than guidance counselors. "But I'd like to point out that it was not my choice."

"Boys. Ryan, Kevin. Hand me the hat," Kook demanded. He held out his hand to Ryan.

"Step away from the hat," Patrick said in a deep voice.

The Gods suddenly handed over the hat, then headed into the cafeteria without saying anything else.

Laurie started to explain what had happened, but Kook cut her off. "I'm on my way to lunch and I don't really want to get into it. Wearing hats is against the school rules, so I'd suggest saving it for after-school wear," Kook said.

That was even funnier to me. Picturing Patrick running out of school with the hat on, as if he were happy to be free just so he could now wear his green plastic hat. I couldn't stop laughing, picturing him running and jumping into the air and clicking his heels together.

Then I saw that Kook was watching me. He had a worried look on his face.

That's when I realized that I was laughing too loud. I was laughing so hard that I had started to cry, and I hadn't even realized it until now. I slid down the wall and sat on the floor on top of my backpack. I tried to stop laughing but I couldn't, and tears were running down my face.

"Alison, are you okay?" Kook said.

"I'm—" I tried to talk, but I couldn't. This was so embarrassing. I was sitting on the floor, laughing and crying, right outside the cafeteria. People were walking in and out. They were probably watching me.

Kook crouched in front of me. "Are you all right?"

"No," I said, giggling and wiping the tears off my face. "I mean, yes, I'm fine, it's just *funny*, that's all." But I couldn't even get the sentence out and have it make sense. What was happening to me? Why couldn't I stop?

"Alison, you know where to find me if you need me," Kook said, standing up. "I'm sorry I have to run, but we have a faculty lunch meeting."

"Do they make you eat fish sticks, too?" Patrick asked him.

That made me laugh even harder. Kook just glanced at Patrick and then me before walking down the hall toward the faculty lounge.

"Who was *that*?" Patrick asked.

"That's the infamous Coach Kook," Laurie said. "Actual

name: Jerry Cucklowicz."

"What does he do, besides break up hat fights?" Patrick asked.

"Oh, well." Laurie shrugged. "Not much." She looked at me as if she were wondering whether to explain what made Kook want to look after me. "He's the wrestling coach. And he just . . . he claims to counsel people. He's Mister Mental Health. I don't know if he's a real psychologist, but he plays one on TV."

"Since when is laughing a problem?" Patrick held out his hands and pulled me up from the floor.

"He hates to see people actually *enjoying* themselves. That worries him." Laurie put my bag over her right shoulder. Then they each got on one side of me, we all put our arms around each other's shoulders, and we walked down the hall together.

"Can you believe how upset they got over a hat? They have hat issues," Laurie said. "And another thing. Why do the best-looking guys have to be so obnoxious? Present company excluded. Of course."

"Of course," Patrick said. "Well, see, it's, um, genetic. The obnoxious gene."

They both kept babbling for the next five minutes, giving me time to recover. My stomach muscles hurt from laughing and I was embarrassed about what had happened. Kook wasn't going to let that go without some sort of note in my record. And what would it say? Crying over a dropped hat?

CHAPTER TEN

"You girls . . . well, you call me when you're ready to leave. Don't accept any rides home from anyone else. Promise me." Mrs. Kuzmuskus was leaning out the window of her car, stopped at the end of Patrick's driveway. The driveway was filled with cars on each side of it, and cars were parked out on the road as well. I could hear music and voices coming from out back, near the barn, where Patrick had said the party would be. I couldn't believe it was so crowded already—we weren't even that late.

"What if it's a date potential?" Laurie asked. "Because you told us to find dates a couple of weeks ago. You insisted on it, if I remember right. 'Will you girls find a date already?' Isn't that what you said?"

"And in those outfits, you just might." Mrs. K. smiled at me.

"Hey, you're the one who told us to dress up, to make an occasion out of it. You're the one who made us raid your closet. Now we look like time travelers from the seventies."

"It's Patrick's fault, actually," I said. He had told us— had told everyone—to "wear something interesting, for once." He'd posted a sign for the party outside the cafeteria—for a half hour, until a teacher saw it and pulled it down—that said, BE ORIGINAL. NOTHING FROM THE GAP ALLOWED IN THE DOOR.

Laurie was wearing an orange nylon halter top of her mom's with straps that tied around the back of her neck, like a swimsuit, and tight black flared polyester pants. She had platform macramé sandals on, which she could hardly walk in. I had a maroon leotard top, a scarf around my neck, a wraparound skirt with a loud block pattern, and black strappy sandals with four-inch heels. For some reason, I was also wearing a black hat with a tall white feather angling backward from the brim. I'd borrowed all of it from Laurie and her mom, who insisted that I looked cool. Instead I looked old, somehow. I looked ridiculous, actually.

"I think you look like Charlie's Angels—the originals. Which is why I'm telling you. Just don't get in someone else's car tonight." Her tone was different from usual, as if she were expecting us to get in trouble or do something dangerous.

"Yes, Mom," Laurie said in a sarcastic voice. "Of *course*, Mom. Whatever you *say*, Mom."

"Laurie, please. I'm serious," Mrs. K. insisted.

"It's okay if you're serious, Mom, just as long as we're not," Laurie said. I realized she was quoting Patrick. She was doing that a lot lately.

Her mother just stared at her. "What? What's that supposed to mean?"

"Don't worry so much. It's a *party*. We'll have fun. We'll call you when we're not having fun," Laurie said.

"Or before," I added.

"Okay. But don't drink," Mrs. K. told us. "Or smoke."

"Just to play it safe, Mom, we'll skip the peanuts, too. In case we're allergic and nobody told us yet. *Bye*." Laurie started walking toward the barn, so I waved good-bye to Mrs. K. and followed her.

I felt ridiculous, walking around in such high heels, wearing such a huge hat. "Why am I wearing this hat again?" I asked Laurie.

"Because Mom wore it for Halloween once and I loved it so much I adopted it. And because we feathered your hair and the feather is a theme. You know what? You do look like someone in an old TV show—or movie." Laurie stopped outside the wide door of the barn to dab some shiny pink lip gloss on her lips. "I know what it is—you look like a pimp."

"I do not!" I said. "Anyway, a girl can't be a pimp."

"Sure she can," Laurie said. "From now on, I'm going to call you Pimpalicious. That's your new name. Pimpalicious."

"Don't," I said, reaching for the lip gloss.

"No, wait. You're right. That's all wrong," she said.

"Yes, it is."

"I'll call you *Miss* Pimpalicious."

"No! It sounds like I have a lot of pimples," I protested.

"Right. But you don't have any. See? That's the beauty of it. It's ironic. That's why I hate you sometimes."

"You hate me?"

"Yeah. You're so lucky."

Lucky. Me? How could she say that? Of all the words I could use to describe myself, that would definitely be the last one I'd choose.

"Oh, God. *Look* at everyone!" Laurie said.

"We're late," I said. "We're like the last people here." I looked around the barn. There must have been over a hundred people inside, talking, laughing, dancing. Almost every sophomore I could think of was there, and about half the rest of the school, too. I saw Dave standing by the stereo, dressed completely punk with his hair sculpted into a Mohawk, and Kelley, wearing a jungle-pattern shirt, khaki pants, and giant parrot earrings. There was one girl wearing a cheerleader uniform, another in a bikini, and even a guy wearing a plaid kilt.

It was like Halloween in March, as if we'd all missed the holiday the first time around and were trying to make up for it now.

"Hey, there's Patrick! Oh, my god. Look at him. He's wearing the hat!" Laurie said excitedly.

I laughed as I saw the green plastic hat perched on Patrick's head. Laurie and I half walked and half stumbled through the scattered leftover hay on the barn floor over to where he was standing by a giant punch bowl. He had on a shiny silver shirt, wire-frame blue sunglasses, and black polyester pants.

"Hey! You're finally here!" Patrick's face lit up and he grabbed my arm.

"You look like a disco leprechaun," I told him, pointing to the green hat.

"How many polyesters died to make that thing?" Laurie reached out to touch Patrick's shirt.

"Oh. Like *your* clothes are environmentally correct?" Patrick stepped back to check out our outfits and lowered his rectangular glasses. "Hm. You're looking very—"

"Trapped in the seventies. I know. It's my mom's stuff. But what's with the disco music?" Laurie asked. "I mean, I love 'YMCA' as much as the next person, but . . . "

"It's Dave. You have to bring it up with him. I had no idea when I asked him to DJ that he had this love of disco music. Maybe he knew what you were going to wear." He squeezed my arm and that was when I realized he was still holding on to me.

I gently moved my arm out of his grasp. "Yeah. Maybe."

"So, you guys want to dance?" Laurie asked.

Patrick and I looked at each other, and then at her. "Um, not yet," I said.

"Not really," Patrick said.

"Come on. You're dancing." Laurie pulled us both by

the elbows, and we followed her reluctantly over to the area in front of the speakers where about forty people were dancing.

"So, your dad's cool about having this many people here?" I asked, speaking loudly so he'd hear me over the music.

"Sure!" Patrick shrugged.

"Come *on*. Quit talking, let's dance!" Laurie shouted as Dave put on a new song. Laurie pulled us both toward her, and the three of us started to dance.

Patrick came up to me and tried to spin me around, but our arms got tangled up and we just started laughing. Laurie hit her hips against Patrick's and they started doing coordinated moves, as if they were on the school dance squad—only they must have dropped out after the first rehearsal, because they ran out of moves thirty seconds later and just started jumping around.

I went outside to get some air about half an hour later and saw the Gods standing by the metal bathtub full of sodas buried in ice. They hadn't dressed up for the event, which didn't surprise me. I couldn't believe they were here, considering they didn't really know—or seem to like—Patrick. But, when you had a party around here, people came whether they were invited or not.

"Hey," Kevin said. He was eating from a bag of Wise potato chips. "Kuzmuskus in there?"

I nodded. "Last I knew, she was dancing."

"This I gotta see. Come on, McGowan." They tossed a couple of cans into a nearby trash can and went inside, leaving me and Ryan alone.

"Wow. You look incredible," Ryan said, walking around me in a circle. "How come you don't dress like that more often?"

"That's a really stupid question," I said.

"Yeah. I guess it is." Ryan laughed. "Nice hat." He reached up and touched the white feather. "A little nicer than that green one. But then, you could make anything look good."

"I doubt that," I said. I started to walk back inside, but my spiked heels sank into the ground, and I stumbled, trying to catch my balance.

Ryan reached out and put his hands on my waist. "Hey, where are you going?"

"Back inside?" I said. Wasn't it obvious?

"Hang out here for a while," Ryan said. "It's so hot in there. Plus we can't drink in there, because certain people would go ballistic and call the cops. So what do you say? Want a beer?" As he loomed closer to me, I smelled the stale beer on his breath—mixed with the smell of cinnamon, because he was chewing cinnamon gum, like he always did.

"Come on, try some," Ryan urged me. "It's not like you've never had a beer before."

I glared at him. I couldn't believe he would bring up that night. I drank with him, too much, until I cried and cried, and the next day I cut things off with him completely.

"Just a couple of sips. It'll make you feel better," Ryan said. He put his arm around my shoulders, and I leaned away from him, away from the cinnamon-beer smell.

"No, it won't." I knew that for sure. "No. *Ryan.*" He was tilting the beer can toward my lips.

"Alison?" Patrick called from the barn door. He walked over to us. "Why don't you leave her alone?" He pulled at Ryan's arm, and the beer can he'd been holding up to my mouth dropped to the ground. Beer sloshed up and out, drenching the grass, splashing onto my feet.

"Why don't *you* shut up?" Ryan replied, stepping back from both of us. He stared at Patrick and then at me. "You're such a freak, Alison. Why do you hang around him?"

"Why shouldn't I?"

"Because I don't get it. I don't understand why you spend so much time with him. You're gorgeous. You're beautiful. He's—a jerk."

"Actually, he's not the jerk," I said.

Patrick stepped up to Ryan. "She doesn't want your stupid beer. She doesn't want your arm on her shoulders. Okay? Isn't it obvious?" he asked.

Ryan shoved him. "What do you know? You don't know her the way I do. Get away from me."

"How about *you* get out of here?" Patrick replied.

And then before I could do anything, Ryan drew his arm back and punched Patrick right in the face. His tinted sunglasses smashed into his nose and then broke and fell to the ground.

Patrick stood there, just blinking and stunned for a second, and then he grabbed Ryan's arms and wrestled with him, trying to push him back. They were still scuffling when there was a loud, air-piercing whistle. Instinctively they both stopped and looked up, as if this were a wrestling match and a penalty had been called.

"What's going on?" Laurie was standing in the wide barn doorway. "Patrick Kirkpatrick, what the hell are you doing now?"

"Do you have any frozen vegetables?"

Mr. Kirk just stared at Laurie when she walked into the kitchen. He was standing by the sink, sipping from a glass. He wore a polo shirt and jeans, and his sandy brown hair was longer than Patrick's and slicked back. "Why, are you hungry?" he asked.

"No, they're not for me," she said. "They're for him." She gestured over her shoulder at Patrick, who was just coming in the back door.

Mr. Kirk frowned at Patrick. "What happened? What have you done now?"

"Dancing injury," Laurie said. "Unbelievable coincidence. Patrick was moving like this"—she demonstrated a dance move—"and someone else was moving like this, and then—wham! Right in his face."

"Dancing is a lot more dangerous than it looks," I added.

Mr. Kirk shook his head, not falling for our story. "Unbelievable. Do I have to teach you how to fight?" He examined Patrick's swollen face and quickly ran a paper towel under the faucet, then wiped away a few drops of blood coming from Patrick's nose. "You said a few dozen people were coming. A small get-together, you said."

"Word gets around," Laurie said. "People are like desperate around here for parties."

"Yes. Well. Help yourself to the frozen foods." Mr. Kirk tossed the wet paper towel into the trash can. "I'm going to run out and check on everyone, make sure no other fights are breaking out." He gave Patrick another cold glance before he left. "I can't believe you sometimes."

We all stood there for a second and pretended that hadn't just happened.

Then Laurie opened the freezer and rooted around inside. "Mixed veg would be okay, but peas are the best," she said.

"Have you gotten that many black eyes?" Patrick asked. Under the overhead fluorescent kitchen light, the skin under his eye looked painfully swollen already, and his nose was puffy.

"Not me," Laurie said. "My dad. Years ago."

"Really?" I asked. I'd forgotten that, if I ever knew.

"Oh, yeah. My mom hated peas, but we always had them around. Aha!" Laurie pulled out a bag of frozen green beans. "Not great, but they'll work."

Patrick stared at the bag, puzzled. "I didn't know we had French-style green beans."

"Hold them," Laurie told him, "like this." She pressed the bag against his nose and face. Then she helped him over to the counter and guided him to sit down on a stool.

I decided to leave them alone for a few minutes, so I went back outside. I went around to the front of the house to see if Ryan had left yet. I didn't see him or his truck anywhere, so I sat down on the front porch steps. A few minutes later, Patrick came out of the house.

"Where's Laurie?" I asked.

"Bathroom," he said.

"Ah."

Patrick sat next to me and rested his elbow on his leg, keeping the green beans against his face. "I don't think I'll have another party any time soon."

"Really?"

"Yeah. I don't do all that well at parties. In case you couldn't tell." He shifted the bag slightly and leaned against me, his shoulder resting against mine.

I felt myself go tense and rigid at first, but then I told myself to relax. I leaned back against him. "Yeah, well, I haven't been to a party in such a long time, I can't even remember how I do," I confessed.

Patrick laughed. "Ouch. Don't make me laugh. My face hurts."

"Okay." And we just sat there leaning against each other.

A few minutes later, I heard the screen door close. I quickly moved away from Patrick, making room for Laurie to sit down between us.

"You weren't lying. Your dad *is* a serial flirt. I went into the kitchen to grab a soda and he wouldn't stop talking to me," she said as she opened a can of root beer.

"As long as he doesn't ask you out," Patrick said.

We both stared at him, horrified. "He wouldn't," I said.

"No. He likes older women," Patrick said. "You know, twenty-year-olds."

Laurie laughed. "Okay, so we're safe. For a few more years at least."

"So. Should we go back over there and dance?" I asked. "Or something?"

"No. I'd rather hang out here," Patrick said, the green beans crunching as he shifted the bag again on his nose and face. The beans were starting to thaw a little, and water was dripping onto Patrick's shirt.

"Yeah. Me, too," I said. Over in the barn, dance music was blaring, and everyone seemed to be having a great time. And here we were, outside, and for once I didn't feel like I was missing anything.

CHAPTER ELEVEN

The next morning Laurie was already in the kitchen, starting to make breakfast, when I got out of bed. She had made a pot of coffee and was getting the frying pan out from underneath the stove when I walked into the kitchen.

Mrs. K. wasn't up yet, but I wasn't surprised—she'd gone out with friends after picking us up from Patrick's and dropping us off here. I hadn't even heard her come home, so it must have been late when she did.

Suddenly Laurie swore and started rubbing her shin. "What's wrong?" I asked.

"I couldn't get this stupid pan out because it was stuck under a stack of like six others, and then I hit myself with it." She pressed lightly on her leg. "That is going to be so black and blue, it's not funny."

"You hit yourself with a pancake griddle?" I tried not to laugh, but I couldn't help it.

"Okay, not all that funny," she said, shooting me an angry look.

"Sorry," I said. "How about if I make them?"

"No, that's okay. I can do it." She limped over to the cabinet and got out a measuring cup. "How many should I make? Like . . . twelve?"

I shrugged. "I guess so. How come you're up so early?"

"I couldn't sleep. You know what I was thinking about? This is going to sound whiny. But it's like, you have guys *fighting* over you. And sometimes I feel like I'm not even here. No one gives a crap about me."

"What? Don't say that. That's not true," I said.

"Alison, come on. When it comes to guys, I'm invisible."

Was that what she thought? "Are you kidding me? Invisible?" I thought of the way the Gods had teased her the night before, how she had teased them right back. "They all think you're so great. What are you talking about?"

"Yeah. They think I'm great because they like me as a friend. Like a guy friend. They want to be my buddy or pal or whatever." She cracked a couple of eggs and tossed the shells into the trash. "I'm so sick of being everyone's buddy. They wouldn't *fight* to date me." She looked accusingly at me.

"No one's fighting over that," I said. "Ryan was just being obnoxious last night, and Patrick happened to come out before I could get away from him. He was protecting me. You would have done the same thing if you weren't inside doing the electric slide with Jason."

"Oh, yeah. That was fun." She smiled. "He totally

didn't want to dance, but I made him."

"See, I could never do that," I told her.

"But you wouldn't *have* to. Because someone would ask you to dance—they always do."

I didn't know what to say. She was right, in a way. "I don't know, Laur. I think you could get any guy you wanted to," I said. "You're so much more confident than me."

"Are you serious? Everyone's always saying I'm funny or I'm outrageous or I'm cute. But no guy wants cute and funny. Not really. No, I get *leftovers*, if anything. I get guys who want to be my best friend, my buddy. Like the Gods. Like Ryan. He only talks to me because he has to talk to me to get to you now. I'm like your interpreter."

"That's not true. That's not true at all. And you can't say that Patrick thinks you're invisible. You guys were dancing half the night together," I reminded her, feeling slightly uncomfortable because of the way he and I had sat so close for a few minutes. "If the same thing had been happening with you, he would have decked Ryan."

"I don't know. Do you think so?"

"Of course!"

"But it's all hypothetical. We won't ever find out, because Ryan won't ever hit on me like that. Which is fine, I'm over that, and it's a good thing for Patrick's face, but still."

"I bet you'd punch out Ryan yourself before Patrick got a chance," I teased her.

"Yeah, but there's a problem with not being able to reach his face." Laurie jabbed the air above her. "My reach is no good."

Mrs. K. shuffled down the hall from her bedroom in her slippers. "Girls, could you keep it down? Some of us are trying to sleep."

She half staggered toward the coffeemaker, grabbed a mug from the cupboard, and poured herself a cup. She leaned against the counter, set her mug on it, and rubbed her eyes. "So what are you arguing about now?" she grumbled.

"We're not arguing, we're discussing. There's a difference," Laurie said.

Mrs. K. sipped from her coffee mug and waited for us to explain. But we didn't. She rubbed her temples with her fingers. "So. What's for breakfast?"

"What do you think?" Laurie snapped. "Pancakes. Blueberry if you're lucky."

Mrs. K. looked at me and raised an eyebrow. "She *is* in a good mood, isn't she?"

I had just picked up a spare and cried, "Yes!" when I heard applause behind me. I turned around, expecting to see my dad giving me a hand, all excited because *I* was, for once. But instead, it was Patrick who was clapping. He was standing behind Sam, dressed in baggy black shorts and a bright-colored cycling jersey, and he was carrying a bike helmet under his arm. When he took off his wraparound sunglasses, I saw that his cheek was purple and bruised. The bowling alley lights didn't exactly flatter it.

"Hey, what are you doing here?" I asked, hopping down the step from the lane.

"You said you'd probably be bowling this afternoon, and I was out for a ride," Patrick said. He ran his hand through his short hair, which was a little spikier than usual from sweat. He didn't get helmet hair, apparently. He was blessed with thick hair, the opposite of me.

"You bowl?" Sam asked excitedly.

"No, the hand-eye coordination thing . . . it pretty much carries over into everything." Patrick slid into one of the plastic seats behind the scoring table.

"Is that how your face ended up like that?" my dad asked. "Due to a lack of coordination?"

"Actually, that had more to do with my mouth." Patrick shrugged.

"Was this related to that party last night?" my father asked. He looked over at me. "You didn't mention any fights. Actually, you didn't mention anything about last night."

"Oh, it wasn't a fight, Mr. Keaney," Patrick said. "It was a minor scuffle. It was one of those things that was over before it began."

"You lost," Sam said bluntly.

"Possibly." Patrick propped his feet on another chair. He was wearing cycling shoes that had metal tips on the end to attach to the bike's pedals.

"So you can't bowl in those shoes," Sam told him.

"I don't think I can bowl, period," Patrick said. "But I'm going to watch. You guys go ahead. Maybe I'll learn something."

"You're up, Dad." Sam cleared our last game's score, while I sat down beside Patrick.

"So I was thinking Birch Bowl sounds like a takeout Thai place," he said. "You know, one of those places where you can get pan-fried noodles or pad thai or pick your own vegetables and sauce and rice and they just wok it right in front of you."

"Um . . . no?" I said.

"Boston. We'll go," Patrick said. "Next chance we get."

"Right," I said. But I knew that I probably wouldn't, that it was highly doubtful.

"So check it out. Look what I just found at Salvage City for you." He reached behind his back and pulled something out of the pocket on the back of his jersey. "It probably doesn't even play all the songs, but it was only seventy-five cents."

He handed me a CD in a slightly crushed jewel case. It was a compilation of disco songs. "Thanks," I said. "But . . . " Why was he bringing me a disco CD?

"I thought you might want to practice your hustle," Patrick said.

My father turned around from the scoring table. "Practice her what?"

122

"Dancing. We were dancing last night," I told him. "You know, disco."

"Disco duck," Patrick sang. "Quack quack."

"Don't remind me." Dad turned back around.

"So that was kind of freaky last night," Patrick said in a quieter tone. "The Neanderthal thing."

"Hey, you going to bowl with us or not?" Sam asked. "Come on, get some shoes."

"Okay," Patrick said. "But no making fun of my game."

"Don't worry. I'll be too busy making fun of the fact you shave your legs," Sam said.

I checked out his legs. They were strong-looking, tan, and muscular—and very, very smooth. Why hadn't I noticed that before?

"Is that to make you faster or something?" Sam asked.

"No, that's sort of a myth. It saves you like a hundredth of a second, but that's it. The reason lots of cyclists do it is because it cuts down on road burn—if you get injured, it's not as bad," Patrick explained. "You heal faster after you crash."

"Oh, yeah? So you crash a lot?" Sam asked.

"Your brother is a riot," Patrick said dryly as he went up to rent shoes from Rick.

We'd played two games when Dad finally gave in to Sam's begging and agreed to go buy us sodas. Even though Patrick was an even worse bowler than Sam, we were all having a really good time, and I was starting to feel a little guilty because I should have called Laurie and told her to come down and meet us. She wouldn't want to miss out on this, with Patrick here. But Dad had insisted we could only afford one more game, and we'd decided to make it "all or nothing." Whoever won would be considered the best bowler of the day. It was sort of silly, because we all knew it was going to be Dad, unless he felt sorry for us and threw the game.

Patrick flopped down behind the scoring table while we waited for our sodas. He crossed his arms on the table and rested his head on them. Then he looked over at me. "You know, I think I just realized why I suck at bowling. Check out the pins. It's a triangle. You have to hit the pins at a certain angle. It's all freaking geometry."

I started laughing, and then out of the corner of my eye, I saw Dad talking to a woman over at the snack bar. They were standing too close to each other. She was perched on a stool, and Dad was sort of semi-leaning against the back of the chair beside her.

I hadn't even noticed her come in. How long had she been here? Was Dad only getting us drinks because that gave him an excuse to go over there? Was he learning to flirt now?

"Hey, Alison. You're scowling. What's the matter?" Patrick asked.

"She gets like this," Sam said. "She hates to lose."

"That's not why," I said slowly. I kept looking at my

father, wondering who that woman was and when he was going to leave her alone and come back to us.

Patrick followed my gaze for a second, then said, "Hey, Sam, Alison. You ever tried speed bowling?"

"What's that?" Sam asked.

"We all bowl at the same time. You race to see who knocks down pins first. You get points if you hit the other person's bowling ball, too. It's sort of like croquet."

"There's no such thing as speed bowling," Sam said.

"Come on, I'll show you. Come on." Patrick hopped up onto the lane and took a bowling ball from the rack. "You take one, too," he told Sam. They both walked back to the edge, so they could take several steps before the foul line. "Ready? Set? Go!"

They sprinted to the foul line and dropped the bowling balls, which collided halfway down the lane and were knocked into the gutters.

"Lane five—what are you doing?" Rick said over the public address system. "Stop that please."

They each grabbed another bowling ball right away; and this time, Patrick and Sam pushed and shoved each other as they made their approach. The two bowling balls cruised down the lane side by side. Then pins were crashing down and Patrick was yelling, "Speed strike!" and Sam was high-fiving him and claiming to have knocked down more pins.

"Lane five, I repeat. Stop that!" Rick called.

"Come on, Alison. You've got to try it, too," Patrick said. "It's even better with three people." As soon as the pins were reset, he took another bowling ball for himself and handed one to me. "This time, no pushing. Speed only." Sam grabbed a bowling ball and the three of us lined up.

"Ready . . . go!" Patrick said.

We all started to run, but Patrick and Sam pushed right past me, bowled, and then Patrick put his arms around mine to keep me from throwing the ball, while Sam blocked the lane with his body. We were laughing and at the same time, I was squirming to get out of Patrick's grip—he had his arms around my waist, and he was almost hugging me, and it felt like we shouldn't be that close, like this was something you did with a boyfriend, not just a friend.

Rick came jogging over. "Stop that right now or I'll kick you out. You're breaking the rules. Candlepin has very strict rules!" He was panting from the effort of moving so fast. He was more of a behind-the-counter guy.

"Sorry," Sam said, as Patrick released me, and we both exchanged awkward glances and took an extra step away from each other.

"I'll have to ask you to bowl somewhere else if you ever do that again," Rick said. "And I mean it, Sam, Alison." He glared at Patrick. "And whoever you are."

"It won't happen again," Patrick told him as I put the unused bowling ball back in the rack.

"Uh-huh. See that it doesn't. Don't wear out your welcome." Rick hitched up his pants, turned around, and walked back over to his desk.

"Candlepin rules," Patrick scoffed. "Hasn't he ever heard that rules are made to be broken?"

"What's going on?" Dad asked as he rushed back with a tray of sodas.

"We almost got kicked out of the Birch Bowl. Cool!" Sam laughed.

"You *what?*" Dad asked, looking appalled.

"Patrick was showing us a different style of bowling. That's all," I explained. "Rick hadn't heard of it yet."

"Yeah, well, news travels slow around here, what can we say? But I'd better get this out of here before Rick yells at *me*, and he would, too." Dad walked back and carefully set the tray on a square table behind the bowling area, which was the only area Rick allowed you to eat and drink. You had to finish a frame, run up, drink something, and then run back.

Patrick leaned next to me at the table as we both picked up our sodas. He was standing so close to me that I felt uncomfortable.

"So, who's ready for all or nothing?" Dad asked.

"I'm going to go call Laurie first," I said, as I backed up from the table toward the pay phone. "She should be here."

"But she hates bowling," Dad said. "And this is our last game."

"So, maybe she wants to meet us afterward," I said.

"We don't have to do everything with Laurie. Do we?" Patrick asked me.

"Actually, yes, you do," Dad said. "They are attached at the hip, you know."

Normally I'd hate him for interrupting like this and bringing up the "attached at the hip" comment. But right now it was okay. He was right; Laurie should be here. Because I didn't feel like I should be alone with Patrick, not the way things were going.

"Well, then, definitely. Let's call Laurie." Patrick smiled. He pulled a cell phone out of his jersey's back pocket and tossed it to me. "I take this on rides in case of emergency."

It wasn't an emergency, but it was somehow urgent. While I talked to Laurie, I stuffed the disco CD from Patrick into my bag. I didn't want Laurie to find out about it, for some reason.

CHAPTER TWELVE

"So, the reason you've been hanging around all year has arrived," Mr. Garcia announced at our next journalism class. "It's time for the yearly high school newspaper conference in Boston."

"Yes!" Laurie pumped her fist into the air. "*Finally.*"

Mr. Garcia handed a stack of orange paper to Kelley, who glanced at the top sheet and then handed them around the table to each of us. "Here's most of the information. I need everyone who wants to go to sign up, and then I need a permission form back from your parents and a check to cover a few expenses."

"How will we get there?" Patrick asked.

"By bike, naturally," Laurie said. "Actually, *we're* flying in the private Birch Falls High jet—"

"The *High Bugle*?" Patrick asked.

"And *you're* riding your bike," Laurie finished.

Mr. Garcia cleared his throat. "We're taking one of the school vans. And, yes, in case you're wondering, we'll have another adult chaperone with us, so I can keep an eye on all of you. I know it's only a hundred miles, but who knows what kind of trouble you guys could cause in that short span of time. Not to mention when we get there."

"What I *really* love about you is the way you trust us," Laurie said. "That and your shoes, of course."

Mr. Garcia smiled. "Now, my sister has strangely offered us the use of her town house apartment this year. I tried to explain that she doesn't know you yet, but"—he shrugged— "she insists. It means sleeping on the floor—she's got a couple of couches as well—but it's a lot cheaper than renting hotel rooms. Is everyone okay with that?"

"That depends," Kelley said. "Do I get the sofa or the floor?"

"Hallway," Patrick muttered under his breath.

"We'll draw straws," Mr. Garcia said. "I'll be handing out a sheet with a detailed itinerary in a few days, for both you and your parents to look over, make sure everything's copacetic."

"Okay, so what stories do people have for this week?" Kelley asked.

"I had a brainstorm." Patrick sat up straighter in his seat. "April Fools' is coming up."

"And? That's news?" Kelley asked.

"*And*, I was thinking that maybe instead of a regular edition of the paper, we should do a joke one," Patrick said. "I mean, we'd be passing up a huge opportunity to make fun of people if we didn't."

"That's not what a school paper is supposed to do," Kelley said. "In fact, I think it's part of the charter that we're not allowed to do that."

"That can't be right," Laurie said. "I'm sure someone, sometime, did a joke edition of the *Bugle*. It's been around a long time. No offense, Patrick, but you can't be the first person who's thought of it."

"*I've* never seen one," Kelley said, still resisting the idea. "And I never heard anyone like my mom or dad mention it."

"Hm. Well, I for one could use a good laugh," Mr. Garcia said. "What does everyone else think?"

"I'm all for it," Dave said.

"Me, too," added Jason.

"I don't know," Kelley said. "What are we going to write about? What if we offend someone?"

"That's the point," Patrick said.

"No, that can't be the *point*," Kelley said. "Not when I'm editor in chief."

"Kel, as the saying goes, it's all in good fun. As long as we make fun of people equally, no one can complain. Right?" Patrick asked.

"I think he's right, Kelley. But we'd have to discuss all of our articles in advance," Mr. Garcia said. "Especially *yours*, Patrick."

Everyone laughed.

"So we can do it?" Patrick asked.

131

"I think so. Track down a back issue, if you can, Alison. But be careful, everyone. Try to keep things general—you know, like 'School Sold to Pepsi' . . . 'Aliens Take Over Chem Lab and Clone Ms. Flaugherty' . . . only a whole lot funnier than that, I hope. And nothing about compromising positions," Mr. Garcia said.

"Compromising positions?" Kelley asked.

"He means sex," Patrick said, smiling at her.

"Oh." Kelley's face turned red. "Well, of course not."

"I'm going to write a column called 'Kissing Cousins,' only I'm spelling 'cousins' with a k-u-z. And I'll make up a bunch of inflammatory gossip about people, especially people who are related. 'Kay?" Laurie asked Mr. Garcia.

"Um, no. *Not* . . . 'kay," he told her. "Think of something else."

Laurie sighed loudly. "If I have to."

"Hey, if it's scandal you want, I'll volunteer," Patrick said. "What do you say, Kelley? You in?"

"No." She frowned at him. "You're asking the wrong person."

"Oh. Well, who *is* the right person?" Patrick looked around the table at everyone. When he got to me, he started to smile. "Alison? Of course this would be all in the name of good journalism. Naturally."

I felt Laurie looking at me, and I wished Patrick hadn't said anything. Don't do that, I wanted to tell him. Don't flirt with me.

"Patrick, no offense, but you haven't *done* any good

journalism yet," Mr. Garcia said, laughing.

"Oh. What a blow." Patrick gripped his shirt, right over his heart. "Mr. Garcia. That's harsh."

Laurie had a dentist appointment that afternoon, so her mother picked her up, and I walked home by myself. One of my favorite places in town was the long, narrow bridge that crossed the river above the falls. On the bus or in a car, you barely noticed the falls because you were right on top of them and you couldn't look straight down—the bridge got in the way, and besides, the falls weren't exactly huge. But walking, you could peer over the edge and listen to the rushing water, which was really loud this time of year. It was a soothing sound, in a way.

I was halfway across the bridge when I heard someone yell, "Hey!" I turned around and saw Patrick coming up behind me on his bike. He wasn't riding as fast as he usually did, and he was wobbling a little, trying to stay on the narrow sidewalk.

My hair was whipping in my face, so I waved hello and then turned back around so that it would blow out behind me. Patrick coasted up, got off his bike, and leaned it against the metal railing. He came up to me and stayed a few feet back from the railing at first. "How can you stand it up here? I feel like I'm going to get blown over the edge. I usually go like ten miles out of my way so I don't have to ride over this bridge."

"The railing will hold you. It's safe," I said, shaking it

to show him how sturdy it was. Below us, the river pooled and swirled before the water rushed over the falls. I reached into my bag for a ponytail holder and roughly smoothed my hair into a short ponytail to get it out of my face. I was so sick of growing my hair out I could scream.

"Bridges like this make me nervous," Patrick said, stepping a little closer to the edge now.

"Don't worry, you'll get used to it," I told him. "You know, you'll have to get used to it by senior year. People jump off. It's a ritual."

"Everyone?" he asked, disbelieving.

"No, not everyone, I guess," I said. "Maybe only a couple, I don't know. But see this?" I leaned over and pointed to a section of metal support underneath, where initials, names, and dates were spray painted.

Patrick looked down at the paint. "Yeah, well, maybe I won't be here then. Maybe I can get out of it."

"Seriously?" I asked. "Why wouldn't you be here?"

Patrick shrugged. "I don't know. Let's just say I haven't stayed in the same place for long lately. I don't exactly have a great track record."

"Oh. Really?" I asked.

"Yeah." He was quiet for a minute, gazing down at the water, gently pushing on the railing to make sure it would hold. A few rust specks came off on his hand. "So, there's something I kind of wanted to talk to you about."

He looked so serious that I felt a little panic inside. I

turned away and stared down at the water, waiting for him to talk, wondering how I could get out of this—whatever it was. Not that I wanted to run away from Patrick, exactly—that wasn't it. I just felt scared.

"I mean, Laurie told me about your mom. What happened last year," Patrick said.

I kept looking at the falls.

"I had no idea. I mean . . . look, I'm really sorry." He sighed. Then he hit himself on the forehead. "That is such a stupid thing to say, I know."

"You do? You mean, from personal experience?" I asked.

"No, it just sounded stupid coming out of my mouth. Like a lot of other things do." Patrick smiled sheepishly.

I would have given anything if he *did* know. If there was anyone in town who knew what it felt like, who could tell me how I was supposed to talk, what I should say to "I'm sorry." "Thank you" seemed ridiculous, but that's what my dad always said, and I didn't get it, I'd never understood it.

There was a really awkward silence between us. I thought he was probably expecting me to tell him about it, but I wasn't going to. A big, loud truck went by on the bridge, which gave us both a chance to recover.

"So anyway. I'm not in the same situation, 'cause I'm just one of the divorce war vets," Patrick said. "But I do know what it's like to live with just your dad—a little bit. I'm learning, actually."

135

"You didn't live with him before?" I asked.

"Well, not since I was nine, and not just the two of us," Patrick said. "When my parents got divorced, my mother and I lived together."

"How was that?" I asked.

"Great. At least for a while. Summers at Dad's, winters at Mom's. It was a regular routine." Patrick lifted his sunglasses and pushed them back on top of his head. "Then I started screwing up and she just couldn't deal with me. So they put me in boarding school for a while, but then I got kicked out, so. This is Plan C, I guess."

At least you have a plan, I wanted to say. At least you still have two to choose between.

"You know what the worst thing was?" Patrick picked up a few pebbles from the bridge sidewalk and tossed them down into the rushing water. "The worst thing was one time when I heard them arguing. I was coming down the stairs and I heard my mom saying, 'Well, *you* take him then.' Like I was a screaming two-year-old or something."

I didn't know what to say. Maybe Patrick didn't know what my life was like. But maybe there were things about his that were almost as bad. "That's terrible. I'm sorry," I said, before I could stop myself from saying that meaningless phrase.

"It's not like I did anything *that* bad, either. She just didn't see it that way."

I glanced over at him. "Should I ask?"

"Should you ask what I did?" Patrick shook his head. "You're better off not knowing." He laughed. "No, don't worry. It was stupid stuff. Like breaking curfew, driving without a license—on a completely deserted country road, mind you. Oh, and I broke into the headmaster's office—except it was a woman and they thought headmistress sounded weird so they called her a 'head.' I mean, how would you like to go through life being called *Head*? Anyway, I went into her office with some other guys and we filled it up with newspaper and glued some things to her desk. You know. Really, really typical boarding school stuff. It was practically in the handbook. No—the brochure."

When he turned to me, I realized I'd been smiling through the whole story, even though in a way it was sort of sad. "So was the getting expelled part in the brochure?" I asked.

"Not exactly." He laughed. "So. How about you? Any trouble with the law?"

"No. Hardly. Well, this one time, in seventh grade, Laurie and I thought it would be cool to steal a bunch of candy from the general store. Actually, it was her idea. She nabbed five 3 Musketeers bars. I got caught when a package of Chuckles fell out of my sock."

Patrick started laughing. "An amateur mistake."

"Yeah. We didn't try it again," I said.

"What did your parents do about it?" he asked. "I mean, your . . . " His voice trailed off.

I made off with a roll of Necco wafers, and my mom had told me she thought that was a really poor choice, that next time I should go for chocolate. "Nothing, really," I said quickly. "I don't remember." I wished I hadn't remembered was more like it.

"Oh." Patrick nodded and pushed against the railing, as if he were testing it. "Every once in a while it's just so tempting. You know?"

I looked at him. "What is?"

"Just to think about causing some trouble—not to actually do anything. Probably." He smiled. "I mean, if I'm in trouble here, it's like—where are they going to send me next? Military school? My grandparents? Actually, that would be cool. But, no, I'm not trying to do anything all that adventurous now. Just like . . . make it to junior year at this point. Pass freaking geometry and biology."

"Short-term goals are good," I said. "I pretty much have it broken down to just getting through this week."

"Is it that bad?" Patrick asked. "I mean, I can imagine how—"

"No," I said quickly. "I was just joking." But then, that was lying. For some reason I didn't feel like covering up and pretending around Patrick. "Some days are so easy, you know, it's like you don't even think about things and you're having a good time and you sort of forget. Then all of a sudden it's Thursday and you just can't take another depressing meal at home. Not that you could call them meals.

Sometimes I think we're the test kitchen for the frozen food industry."

Why was I telling him all this? Why was I confiding in him? I hadn't talked to another person for this long, outside of Laurie, in forever. And it was easier for me to tell him, somehow. Maybe because he didn't know anything, because he hadn't been here, because he didn't know her.

"Are you kidding me? You should see how my dad is about cooking. I make spaghetti three times a week and the other two we go out," Patrick said. "Do you cook?"

I shook my head. "I used to. A little, anyway. But it's not . . . it's not fun anymore."

"Yeah, well, fun is overrated." Patrick was leaning on the railing, and he turned to look at me. The corners of his mouth curled up in a half smile as he slid over and nudged me.

We were standing so close together that he sort of blocked the wind. I felt warmer and protected somehow. It wasn't like having Ryan grab me or hug me—this was different.

And I knew exactly why Laurie was falling for him. There was something really sweet about him, about the way he tried to cheer me up without getting serious, and he was so cute when he sort of flopped down on tables, and even though he wasn't doing that well, he always tried to make everyone else feel better.

But I couldn't take how he was looking at me, how

close we were standing. It scared me to feel that close to someone now. I did everything I could to keep my distance so that I wouldn't feel this, so that I didn't want this. But being with Patrick . . . I did want this. But I couldn't, I just couldn't take the risk. And besides, I knew how Laurie felt about Patrick and that I couldn't feel the same way about him.

"So, you want to go somewhere?" Patrick asked. "Not that this isn't great, but the wind is *totally* ruining my hair. Yours still looks good, though." He reached up and touched my ponytail.

"Not really. Go where?" I asked, backing up a little, turning my head to get the ponytail out of his grasp.

"Beats me. You're the local," Patrick said. "You want coffee or something? Ice cream? Hey, what about that place shaped like a giant cone?"

"I-C Treat. It's closed. I worked there last summer. Paper cap, pink apron, the works."

"Coffee then."

"But let's call Laurie when we get there—she can meet us."

"Oh. Well, yeah, okay," Patrick said. "Call her now, if you want." He handed me his cell phone. I called and left Laurie a message to meet us at the coffee counter inside Frenchy's Candy Kitchen.

"Coffee's only a quarter there and you can hang out as long as you want," I told Patrick as I handed him the phone. "We can work on our ideas for the April Fools' issue. And the key thing is that we can walk from here."

"That is the key thing," Patrick said with a sigh.

I knew I'd somehow irritated him, by wanting to call Laurie, but I couldn't help it. I couldn't be alone with him any longer. Laurie was the one who was falling for him; I was the one who couldn't.

"Come on, let's go. The sooner I get off this bridge, the better." Patrick pointed to my bag, which I'd left on the sidewalk while I stood on the bridge. "That looks kind of heavy. Want me to carry it on my bike?"

"No, it's okay," I said.

"No, look—I can prop it on the back of my bike." Patrick picked up the bag from the ground. "Man! What do you have in here?" he asked as he struggled to attach it to his bike rack. "Shoes? Books? Laptop? Lunch? The kitchen sink?"

"My books and notebooks, that's all. Well, and maybe some other stuff." A three-ring binder. A blank book that I was supposed to write in but never did. A hairbrush and a dozen random, non-functioning barrettes.

"Your shoulders should be bigger, that's all I'm saying. You're stronger than you look." He unhooked a bungee cord from his bike's seat post and wrapped it around the bag to secure it. "Have you heard of these things called lockers?" he asked as we started to walk off the bridge. "Great invention. You leave stuff inside them?"

"I don't use my locker," I said. The sidewalk was barely wide enough for the two of us, so I walked a step ahead of him and the bike. "I actually hate it."

"Really? Why? Wait—you probably have one of those annoying neighbors. You know, so every time you go there, you have to say hi and have a bad conversation."

"No, it's not that. It's a sort of a superstition, I guess, because the last time I did—"

But then I stopped. I felt like I could almost tell him everything right now. And that scared me to death.

I shook my head. "It's a crazy reason. It's just—it's near the chem lab."

"And you're superstitious about getting blown up? Did that happen the last time you were there?" Patrick nodded.

"Sort of," I said.

"Okay. Well, I'll look out for that."

CHAPTER THIRTEEN

"So you'll finish up here?" Mr. Garcia asked. "You'll close up?"

At first Kelley had supervised every single word anyone wrote, and then she got disgusted with all of us and decided she didn't want anything to do with this issue, that she didn't even want her name on the masthead. "Some people can take a joke, and other people . . . well," Mr. Garcia had put it. "But I don't want anyone giving her a hard time about it."

"Too late," Patrick had whispered to me.

"No problem, Mr. Garcia," Laurie said now. "We're all done. We just have to finish printing."

Mr. Garcia stood in the doorway, looking at the three of us, tapping his foot up and down, showing off his latest pair of shoes—blue suede retro sneakers. "I hate to leave. I don't know. Maybe I should stick around."

"What's going to happen? The laser printer's going to attack us?" Laurie joked.

"No, but I told the custodian we'd be out of the building

by eight, and I feel responsible about sticking to that, and it's already seven—"

"Oh, shoot—it's that late?" Laurie looked up from the printer and frowned. "I promised my mom I'd be home by seven for dinner."

"Would you like a ride, Laurie?" Mr. Garcia offered. "And we'll let Alison and Patrick wrap things up?"

"I don't know. Do we trust them?" Laurie looked at me and grinned. She knew she didn't have to worry about leaving me alone with any guy she liked.

Still, normally she would have protested leaving Patrick, I think, but it was Mr. Garcia asking. And we were nearly done. She'd much rather talk to him for a few minutes than sit around baby-sitting a printer and folding over-sized paper in half.

"But how are you going to get home?" Laurie asked me.

I hadn't thought that far ahead. I'd told my dad we'd be here late, and I was sort of counting on Laurie and me leaving together. "Maybe I should go now, too," I said.

"Yeah, but I could use some help folding," Patrick said as he ripped open a new package of paper. "My dad's going to pick me up as soon as I call him—we'll give you a ride home."

"That sounds okay," I said. I looked at Laurie, expecting her to change her mind, to say that she was staying behind, too. But she didn't.

She started to walk out the door, then she turned and gave us a second look. "You guys. You going to be okay?"

"You sound like him." Patrick pointed at Mr. Garcia. "We're leaving here in like half an hour, don't worry."

"Call me!" Laurie said over her shoulder as they headed out the door.

"Me!" Patrick shouted after her. As soon as they were gone, he reached over and pressed the power button on the printer, shutting it off. "No sense wasting any more paper. Man. I thought they'd never leave." Then he reached into his courier bag and pulled out a CD-ROM disk.

"What's that?" I asked. "Why'd you stop printing?"

"This is the real *Bungle*. The extra. I did another layout this morning in study hall. No offense to all the wonderful, hilarious articles other people wrote, but." He glanced at me as he pulled up the file on the computer. "Your piece about Friday fish stick poisoning? That's golden. That's staying. Actually, everything's staying—I'm just adding."

I watched as he launched the file. "But you can't do that."

"Sure I can." He glanced at me and smiled. "It's a supplement, that's all. Some extra material I thought the *Bungle* needed. Trust me, it's going to be great." And then he started repaginating the paper and fooling around with the masthead. I looked over his shoulder as he changed all of our names on the masthead and on our bylines. Laurie Kuzmuskus was now "Sorry, I Must Kiss." Kelley Moroney

145

was "Jelly Donut Moron." Patrick Kirk was "Hat-Trick Jerk." Me? I was "Madison Meanie."

And under Faculty Adviser? It said "Doc Marten, Kenneth Cole, Nike, etc."

Now the paper was six pages long instead of four. There'd be the oversized sheet of paper with pages 1–6 and 2–5, to be folded in half, and then Patrick's supplement, on an $8\frac{1}{2}$"x11" sheet, to stick in the middle and be pages 3–4. He printed a few copies of the center section and handed one to me. "Here, proof this for me, would you? I'll print and fold."

I skimmed through the headlines.

"SMOKER'S RIGHTS RALLY ENDS IN 3-ALARM BLAZE"

"BIRCH FALLS TO GIVE UP FALLS FOR LENT"

"CHEMICAL LEAK SCARE FORCES LIBRARY EVACUATION— ONE PERSON FLEES"

"SCHOOL SPIRIT DAY CANCELED; PRINCIPAL SAYS 'I JUST DON'T CARE'"

I started to laugh, but then I stopped. "Patrick! You can't do this," I said.

"Sure I can. I already did," Patrick said.

"No, really, you can't!" I reached for the stack of papers he was neatly folding in half while the center section printed. "You're going to—you'll get in trouble," I said.

"It'll be funny, people will laugh—don't worry." Patrick tried to get the papers back, but I wouldn't let go. "Come on, Alison. Hand 'em over." He laughed.

"No!" I started to giggle, I couldn't help it. We were fighting over papers we didn't even need, because even as we were arguing over this, more and more copies were printing by the second. Patrick kept pulling at the high stack, which I nearly dropped, but I pulled back. We were looking at each other over the stack we were both tugging.

Then I caught myself. What was I doing? I couldn't do this, not with Patrick. Not with anybody.

I let go all of a sudden, and Patrick lunged toward me, losing his balance, backing me up against the table, dropping the papers to the floor with a loud thud.

I quickly stepped out, away from him. "We should finish up. It's getting late."

"Right." Patrick ran his hand through his hair and leaned over to pick up the sheets from the floor. He stacked them neatly and added the rest of the copies that were still printing. "You mind folding some?"

"No. No problem." I sat down on the other side of the table and glanced up at him as he set a pile in front of me. We smiled awkwardly at each other. "You sure you want to do this?" I asked.

"Yeah. I'm sure," he said. "I'm not worried. You shouldn't be, either."

I just sat there and folded the pages in half, then handed them to Patrick so he could add the supplement.

• • •

"'Sorry, I Must Kiss?'" Laurie just stared at the *Bungle*'s second page and the revised masthead. "What did you guys *do* after I left?"

"Nothing," I said. I remembered the way Patrick had looked at me when he crashed into me, when we were playing tug-of-war.

"What do you mean, nothing?" Laurie asked. And when she said it, I pictured her face peering in the *Bugle* classroom window, watching us last night, misinterpreting that something happened between us. Because nothing happened. And it wouldn't.

"You wrote a whole new section," Laurie said. "This stuff wasn't even in there when Mr. Garcia and I left. The whole thing was four pages, not six!"

"It wasn't me!" I said.

Laurie leafed through the paper, skimming the new pieces. "I mean . . . it's funny. It's hilarious. But Kelley's going to kill us," Laurie went on, not even listening to me. "Mr. Garcia's going to kill us."

"It was Patrick," I said.

I scanned the articles as I walked, carrying a stack of the papers to be handed out. Now that it was actually coming out, some of the pieces did seem a little more vicious than they had the night before.

"KOOK WINS MR. UNIVERSE TITLE—SHRIMP DIVISION" (by Jason)

"KUZ YOU'RE STUPID, THAT'S WHY" (by Laurie)

"LOCAL ELEMENTARY SCHOOL CHILDREN TEACH SCHOOL JOCKS TO READ" (by Patrick, of course) with a picture of the Gods in their football uniforms superimposed onto a picture from elementary school, where the Gods seemed to be looking up at a couple of little kids holding books.

I didn't even want to think how Ryan, Kevin, and Paul would react to that.

When we got to geometry class, everyone was reading the paper and laughing. But when Mr. Lewis walked into the classroom, he looked upset. His face was red, and he seemed a little frayed around the edges. He didn't even bother to call roll. He snapped open his titanium metal briefcase and pulled out a copy of the newspaper.

"There is a certain rag traveling around school today." He held up the *Bungle*. "This is the most unedited, most unfunny excuse for journalism that I have ever seen."

Patrick looked at me and drew his hand across his throat, as if it were being slit. "Dead," he whispered. "We're dead."

"*You're* dead, you mean," Laurie whispered.

I knew Mr. Lewis was probably referring to the article: "MATH OLYMPICS CANCELED: FRENCH JUDGE CAUGHT DINING WITH COLONEL LEWIS."

A picture of Mr. Lewis from the yearbook had been superimposed onto a photo of Captain Jack's Fish Shack, where Laurie sat in a booth, wearing her old, faded Captain

Jack's T-shirt with a beret perched on her head to make herself look French. The three of us had gone to take the picture two days ago, and I laughed every time I looked at it.

The subtitle read: "THIS JUST IN: FISH POISONING NOW WIDESPREAD IN BAY STATE." I'd written that one and blamed it on Fish Stick Friday.

"I've been talking it over with several faculty members and we think the fairest thing to do would be to write an issue about our friends who put this together." Mr. Lewis stared at Laurie, who was sinking in his opinion for the first time, unlike me and Patrick, who had already sunk to the bottom. "But you know what? It's a funny thing, but we don't actually have the time. Because we're too busy *teaching*. We're too busy molding impressionable young *minds*. I'm very disappointed in you, Ms. Kuzmuskus. In all of you, but especially you."

"But, sir . . . with all due respect. This is a joke," Laurie said. "April Fools' Day tomorrow and all? And we do have free speech on our side."

"Yes. You do. And you also have very poor taste on your side. Chop chop. Get up. You're excused from class."

"Where are we supposed to go?" Patrick asked.

"To the principal's office. They're expecting you."

We all stood up, and everyone was looking at us. Some people were laughing as we went out the door. "Way to go, Kuzmuskus!" someone shouted.

"Isn't this great? We're actually getting called onto the

carpet." Patrick's eyes were shining with excitement as the three of us walked down the hall toward the stairs. I thought about how he'd told me that he liked to get into trouble, how he was sort of missing it. For some reason I didn't feel quite as thrilled to be heading to the principal's office. For one thing, it was only three short steps from that office to Kook's.

"Lewis will never give me a good grade now," I said. "Not that I had much of a shot."

"How about me? I'm the one who let him down," Laurie said. "When you do that to teachers, they hold it against you for life."

"You guys. *I'm* the one with the solid D," Patrick said as we quickly walked down the stairs. "There isn't enough extra credit in the *world*."

In the outer office, the principal's secretary was waiting for us. "Go ahead in," she said, gesturing to the door marked PRIVATE.

Inside Principal O'Neill's office, both she and Mr. Doerfler, the vice principal, were standing behind her desk, conferring. They just stared at us when we walked in, without saying a word. The room was filled with the rest of the *Bugle* staff, and Mr. Garcia was sitting in a chair facing the desk. His arms were crossed in front of him, and he was bouncing his legs up and down nervously.

"Hey," Laurie greeted him. "You, too?"

"They don't believe that this wasn't my idea," Mr. Garcia

said. "You know as part of my job as adviser, I'm supposed to . . . advise. *Against* this sort of thing."

Kelley was glaring at Patrick. "Editor in chief Jelly Donut Moron?" She almost spat the words. "You think that's funny? Why don't you go back to private school or wherever it is you came from?"

"Kel, lighten up." Patrick tried to pat her shoulder, but she reached out and grabbed his hand, twisting it.

"Quit calling me Kel. Why did you have to do this?"

I thought about what he said that day on the bridge, about how he had the urge to stir things up, to cause trouble. How he was running out of options for places to live. How he had bikes A through E, and how he'd already blown through Plans A and B. And I thought of how his father had set all these goals for him, that one of them was "getting off to a good start" here and of the way he'd treated Patrick after Ryan punched his face. As if it were his fault, as if everything were.

"Thank you all for coming," Principal O'Neill said, while Mr. Doerfler closed the door. "Sorry this is a tight fit, but I wanted to get you all here at the same time." She took a deep breath and perched on the edge of her desk. "This is a very serious matter. You've taken liberties here that . . . well, I'm not sure can be justified. And I know you put out a great newspaper for us on a regular basis. And that's in your favor. Still. You've gone a bit overboard here."

"We have the school's reputation to consider. We don't

want people to think that the newspaper staff can just get away with anything," Mr. Doerfler said.

Principal O'Neill nodded. "Exactly. We've been in serious discussion about this for the past hour. And I'm sorry, but we're going to have to suspend you—"

"No!" Kelley cried. She pointed at Patrick. "This is all his fault. Principal O'Neill, it's really all Patrick. All the objectionable stuff was his idea. We would never have done anything like this except—"

"Kelley, you're the editor in chief. How could anything get by without your stamp of approval? And as for you . . ." Principal O'Neill looked at Mr. Garcia.

"What *about* me?" Mr. Garcia stared right back at her, almost as if he were daring her to fire him right there on the spot, almost as if that's what he really wanted.

"We're still debating what to do," Principal O'Neill said. "But your trip to Boston next week? That's been jeopardized. Seriously jeopardized." She nodded and looked around the room. "Maybe you'll think a little more next time before you publish something that's this hurtful to so many people. So, without further ado, there's nothing left to do but hand these out." Principal O'Neill picked up a stack of suspension notices.

I looked at Laurie beside me, and she was looking at Patrick, who was biting his fingernails.

Principal O'Neill was about to hand out the first notice to Kelley, who literally had tears in her eyes, then she smiled and ripped it in half.

"Wh—what?" Kelley murmured.

Principal O'Neill kept smiling. "April fool. Nobody's suspended." She held up the rest of the suspension notices. "These are all blank. It's a *joke*."

And then everyone was laughing and screaming and hugging. It was a giant party. Mr. Garcia was doing a jig around the office with Laurie, and Patrick was dancing with me, saying, "I told you it'd be all right," and Kelley was bowing and giving thanks to the principal. Mr. Garcia announced that he was having a party that night to celebrate, that we should all come over to his house at eight o'clock for cake and ice cream.

"This school is surprisingly cool. I mean, you guys made it out as like . . . boring and torturous. But it's not bad," Patrick said as we walked back upstairs.

"Well, all I can think is . . . you're slow," Laurie teased him. She tried to hip check him into the stair railing. "You haven't figured out yet that it's exactly what we said."

"Or maybe it's just gotten better lately," I suggested as I passed them on the stairs.

"'Cause of Patrick Kirkpatrick?" Laurie scoffed. "You're giving him way too much credit."

"Hey, whose idea was it to do the *Bungle* in the first place?" Patrick said as we rounded the corner on the second floor and nearly walked right into Ryan and Paul.

What were they doing out in the hallway in the middle of second period? Then I remembered: the Gods never had to be anywhere, unlike the rest of us. They had a permanent hall pass. For life.

We tried to walk past them, but they stood in our way, blocking us, like a football play they'd practiced many times.

"Do you think you're funny?" Ryan said to Patrick. "Because you're not."

"I'm not?" Patrick asked.

"Look, I can read. But maybe you won't be able to," Paul said in a threatening voice. He put his hand on Patrick's chest and pushed him backward.

"Quit it, Paul," Laurie said. "You sound ridiculous. Leave him alone."

"Why should I?" Paul said. He and Ryan stared at Patrick as if they couldn't wait to get him alone, as if they'd be waiting for him around school or after school.

"Because. That article. It—it was my idea," I said.

"You? No," Ryan said.

"Yes, it was. We stayed late yesterday—ask anyone," I said. "Patrick and I added some stuff and that was one of the articles." I looked Ryan in the eye as I spoke.

"I don't believe you," he said.

"Why not? Why is that so hard to believe?" I asked.

He glanced at Patrick, then looked at me again. He shook his head. "It's not like you."

"You don't know what's like me and what isn't," I said.

"I used to," Ryan said, stepping closer to me. "I know a lot more about you than you think."

"What are you, stalking her now?" Laurie grabbed my arm by the elbow. "Come on, guys, we have to get back to geometry before Lewis hates us even more."

And the three of us took off. We darted past Ryan and Paul and we ran all the way to the end of the hall and ducked into class.

Mr. Lewis glanced up from his desk when we walked in. "That took long enough."

"We got held up," Laurie told him, panting. "Literally."

"Well, you have . . . " He looked at the clock behind his desk. "Five minutes to complete today's test."

"Test?" Patrick asked.

"Wait. This is another April Fools' thing, isn't it?" Laurie asked. "You know, you really had us going, sir—"

"You have three minutes," Mr. Lewis said. "Starting now. Chop chop. Grab a pencil."

"Tutor. Help me," Patrick whispered as we sat back down at our desks.

"Tutors can only help those who help themselves. And those that can pay large sums in cash," Laurie said as she pulled out a pencil. "But for you I'll make an exception."

"I'll copy off her, and you can copy off me," Patrick whispered to me as he grabbed a pen from his bag. "Here, for strength." He reached over and pressed a Jolly Rancher into my palm. Then he didn't let go, and we just sat there for a minute, hands clasped, staring at the test on our desks in front of us, unable to answer a thing.

Let go, I told myself. Let go before Laurie sees. But I couldn't.

CHAPTER FOURTEEN

I was in my room doing homework that afternoon when the doorbell rang. Sam was still at baseball practice, and Dad was at the office, so I ran downstairs to answer it. I pushed back the curtain and peeked out the living room window and saw a bike leaning against the maple tree out front. I was excited at first to see Patrick, but then I felt this dread coming over me, like something bad was about to happen. Why was he here, on his own?

"Hey," I said as I opened the door. "What are you doing here?"

"That is like this town's version of 'hi.' So I'm not taking it as an insult," Patrick said. He walked past me into the house and flopped onto the sofa. "I thought I could do some work on your bike. Then we could go out to dinner before we go over to Mr. Garcia's for the party tonight."

"Oh. Just us?" I asked, sitting in the big stuffed chair across from him.

"Yeah, just us," Patrick said. He leaned back and adjusted one of the pillows under his head. "One of the hot spots. You know, a step up from pizza or fish. My dad can drive us when he gets off work, or we can ride our bikes over together."

"Well, I can't really afford it," I said. "My dad doesn't give me much of an allowance, and the money I earned last summer is pretty much gone, so . . . you know." I was babbling because I needed to stall, I needed to find a polite way to say no.

"I don't care, Alison. I'll buy," Patrick said.

"Oh. Well, yeah, but . . . my dad's probably expecting me, so . . ."

"I know for a fact you don't like being home for dinner. Your dad's not even here right now, and you hate the food. So why are you lying to me?" He sat up and tossed a pillow toward me.

I caught it and clutched it to my stomach. "What? I'm not lying. He wants us all to have dinner together."

"He wouldn't care if you missed one night," Patrick said.

"Yes, he would," I said.

"God. I can't believe I'm sitting here arguing with you about this. I must be crazy," Patrick said, shaking his head. "I am crazy, right? Everyone says that, so it must be true."

I picked at the chair fabric, at a thread that was hanging off the end of the arm. "Why do you say that?"

"Oh, I don't know. Because I've never actually had to talk someone into being taken out for dinner before," Patrick said. "Because going out is a great concept that you don't seem to get. I mean, I'm wondering. Are you ever going to give me a break?"

"Give you a break? What do you mean?" I asked.

"Alison, come *on*." He sounded really frustrated now. "I can't be any more obvious than I'm already being. Or can I? I mean, do you want me to hold up a sign? Should I rent some ad space in the *Bugle* or start a personals section or something?"

I didn't say anything.

"I know the routine. Next you're going to say that if we *do* go out to dinner, we have to call Laurie and invite her, so the three of us can go together. Right?"

I shook my head, staring down at the floor. "I wasn't going to say that."

"Good. Because in case I haven't explained already, I want to take you out to dinner. Just you," Patrick said. "I want to go out with you. I don't want it to always be you, me, and Laurie."

I didn't know what to say. In a way he was saying exactly what I felt. I knew that was what he wanted, and I'd known that for a while. But it didn't matter, for a few reasons. How could I explain it to him? "Patrick, I'm not . . . I don't . . . " My voice faltered.

"You don't what? You don't like me? You don't have a great time whenever we hang out?" Patrick asked.

"Of course I do. And . . . I do like you." I thought of

how we'd held hands in geometry class, how we'd leaned against each other the night of the party, how we'd hung out on the bridge together, how I could almost tell Patrick everything about how I felt. But mostly I thought of how much that scared me, how I couldn't let that happen. I had to hide behind Laurie, like I always did. And I had to think of what she wanted, of what would make her happy. Because she could go out with him. I couldn't.

"But . . . Laurie *really* likes you," I said.

Patrick shrugged. This didn't seem to surprise him. "Yeah, I know. And that's nice, and I'm flattered, and we're friends and we'll stay friends. But that's it. And that doesn't have anything to do with me and you."

"Yes, it does!" I said. "Because I'd never go out with you, because of her."

"Why not? That's stupid, Alison. I can explain it to her—I'll tell her how I feel," Patrick said. "She might be upset at first, but she'd get over it." He got up from the sofa and walked over to me, and he perched on the arm of the chair where I was sitting. "It's not like we'd be ruining her life."

"No, don't—don't tell her. Because—look, can't we just keep things the way they are now? Aren't we having fun—the three of us?"

"Yes—and no," Patrick said. "We can't just pretend. I can't just pretend we're like best buddies, best friends—"

"But we are," I said.

"No, we're not. Because that's not what I want. So I'm just pretending half the time," Patrick said. "I mean, Laurie's great. But I don't think of her . . . like that. From the beginning, it was you. And you know it."

He didn't say anything, as if he were waiting for me to jump in and talk. But what could I say? Maybe I did know that, in the back of my mind. Maybe I wanted that. And maybe I'd been running both toward that and away from that, from the beginning.

He reached out to touch my hair, his finger running down my neck, making me shiver. But I just sat there, feeling paralyzed.

"Laurie . . . you know, Laurie can take care of herself," he said. "Think about what you want."

I jumped out of the chair and walked to the other side of the room, behind the sofa, opposite him. "I want you to ask her out. Not me. If we can't all stay friends, then, okay, we won't be."

I could feel Patrick staring at me, but I couldn't look at him. "Why?" he asked. "Why won't you even . . . Look, you haven't given me one good reason, Alison."

"Because I'm not—" *Ready* would sound so pathetic. *Interested* would be a lie. I did like Patrick, but he had no idea what I'd be giving up, just to see if things might maybe work out between us. How long would that last? And I'd never get Laurie back. Never.

I couldn't explain to him how I felt, how this was a risk

I just couldn't take. Not even for him.

"Because you're not what? Because you won't go out with anyone. Because it's one of those rules Laurie's always talking about? I mean, that's crazy. You know it's crazy. There's no such thing as rules. You don't make *rules* about other people and how you feel about them."

I didn't know what to say. I could tell him I didn't have rules for this, but was that true? I didn't have rules because this had never happened before, and I had no way of knowing how to deal with it. I could tell him that I really did like him and I was already way too close to him and I couldn't risk getting any closer. Because I didn't want to be close to anyone else. I couldn't handle that, I couldn't let down my defenses because when something bad happened, and it would—it would, I knew that—I'd fall apart. Again. I was barely holding myself together now. I was like the brake light on the back of our Subaru that was being held on by duct tape so that it wouldn't fall off, because Dad didn't want to pay to get it replaced.

"You're not even going to talk to me about it. Are you?" Patrick said. "You're not even going to explain why you won't. You don't think you have to, like you get to live by some other rules, your so-called Alison rules, which make no sense at all, by the way. You think you've managed this whole Patrick Fitzpatrick thing."

"No, I don't," I said. "I don't think that." Didn't he know that I hadn't managed anything at all lately?

"Yeah, you do. You think you have something figured out. Don't you? And you don't," he said. "You don't know anything." He went out and slammed the door behind him.

I went to the window and watched him ride away down the road, going faster and faster until he went around the corner and out of sight. Then I went back upstairs to my room and closed the door.

He was right: I didn't know anything, I hadn't figured out anything. Except that I couldn't handle what was going on.

CHAPTER FIFTEEN

"So I think . . . you know. Things are *developing*. Naturally, of course. With Patrick Kirkpatrick," Laurie said when she called me the next morning.

"What?" I asked. I was lying on my back on my bed, and I sat straight up. I couldn't have been more shocked.

"Well, last night at Mr. Garcia's—he was acting sort of different. You know?"

"Different?" I asked, and then I wished I hadn't.

"He kept kind of . . . I don't know. Getting closer to me. Like we were sitting on the sofa, and I mean, really close, and then Kelley tried to sit down, but it was really crowded and he said, no, we can make room and he pulled me even closer." She laughed. "Unbelievable, right?"

"Yeah," I said quietly, picturing the scene and then trying not to, because it hurt. "Unbelievable."

"So you know what else happened? Kelley actually said maybe Patrick *shouldn't* write sports, because he's really pretty bad at that, and maybe he should take over some of her responsibilities. Whatever that means. You know Kelley, she always makes things sound more important than they are," Laurie said.

"Right," I said. Now I was really regretting that I hadn't gone to the party, that I'd sat at home by myself.

"So he'll get to write about fun things from now on. Kelley said she didn't approve of *how* Patrick did the *Bungle*—did he tell you that he got a *week*'s worth of detention for that from Mr. Garcia? But he said it was worth it, and he and Mr. Garcia are still cool. Anyway, Kelley had to admit that she laughed at everything he wrote. Or almost everything. Not the Jelly Donut Moron. Hey, everyone was disappointed you weren't there, and by the way, I'm still not buying the under the weather excuse," she added.

"I was sick," I said. "In fact, I still feel pretty lousy." At least, that was what I'd told my dad when he came to check on me. And hearing about Laurie and Patrick having such a good time together did make me feel fairly lousy, anyway.

"Uh-huh. Well, why anyone would pass up free cake and hanging out with Patrick is beyond me." She coughed. "So, get this. He actually invited me over to watch a movie tonight—just us. We were going to go out, but then we'd have to get his dad to drive us, and he was totally not into that, so."

"What movie?" I asked, just to make conversation, because I was feeling a little stung. Why was he asking her out? Or was he only asking her to do things as a friend?

"I don't know. Hey, you want to come with me?" Laurie asked.

I could just imagine the look on Patrick's face when I showed up with her. I didn't think he wanted to see me yet—not like that, anyway. Or maybe the problem was that I still needed to avoid him. "No, thanks. It's like . . . just about you guys. That's okay."

"Well, what are you going to do?" she asked. "Saturday night. You can't just stay home and watch *America's Funniest Home Videos* with Sam. Promise me you won't do that."

"I won't. That's on Sunday night, anyway," I said.

She laughed. "Oh, no. How could I forget?"

"Don't worry. I'll think of something. Maybe I'll call your mom," I joked.

"Sorry," Laurie said. "Wait—I don't want you to be all alone—"

"It's okay," I said. "Don't worry about it. Just have fun tonight."

I didn't know how I would spend the time. I didn't want to sit at home, but then, Sam and Dad might not even be around, and I could watch TV by myself. I could always ride my bike somewhere, like down to the launch, to see who was around. That didn't sound like a good idea, though. If I went by myself, I wouldn't have an escape clause ready for Ryan. I couldn't say Laurie was waiting for me. Nobody would be waiting or wondering where I was.

If I hadn't said no to Patrick, I'd be sitting around

watching movies with him tonight, instead of Laurie. He wouldn't be *developing* things with her. I didn't know why I had turned him away like that, I thought.

And then I thought, yes, you do.

The weekend went by so slowly that I was excited when Monday came and the school week began again. I didn't see Patrick, except in class. When he, Laurie, and I ended up at the same lunch table on Tuesday, though, I was glad. I wanted to get past this . . . whatever. This feeling really awkward about what happened. I wanted it to be the three of us the way we used to be.

But right away, things felt strange when Patrick and Laurie sat on one side of the table, and I sat on the other. And they were laughing about something that had happened in the school library yesterday afternoon, but I hadn't been there—Laurie hadn't told me she was staying after school to do detention, too, in sympathy.

It was the school cafeteria Two-for-Tuesday special, which meant you got two hot dogs or two hamburgers, but they were minisized. They were cute, but it was pretty stupid. When Laurie got up to get herself a carton of milk, I looked across the table at Patrick.

"You know what? One Tuesday we should ask them to do, like, one of each. And watch Florence panic, because that would upset the cafeteria universe. Right?" I said.

Patrick squirted ketchup onto a cheeseburger and didn't

look at me. "Don't be funny."

I wasn't sure I'd heard him right. "What?" I asked.

"You're not Laurie. So don't try to be like her." He picked up his cheeseburger and took a bite, just looking past me as if I weren't there. I'd never seen this side of him. I couldn't believe he was sitting there, deliberately hurting me, enjoying it.

What was I doing here with him—with them? I was so not welcome all of a sudden. But that was ridiculous. I'd turned him down a few days ago and now he was in love with Laurie, now he didn't even want to talk to me?

"You guys look like you just got food poisoning," Laurie said as she slid into her seat. "What's wrong?"

Patrick set the burger down and reached for a napkin. "I'm just pissed at my dad. His stupid probation thing. Just because of the *Bungle* detention and because my GPA isn't high enough. Which is only because I can't do geometry. I mean, Alison has a C or whatever and her dad's cool about it, he doesn't make *her* give up her cycling career."

Why was he being funny now that Laurie was back? "That's because he doesn't know I have a C," I said. "I don't tell him everything."

"Big surprise," Patrick said.

I looked at him. What was that supposed to mean?

"You're getting better at it—tell your dad that. You got a D on the last pop quiz instead of an F, right?"

Patrick raised his eyebrow. "He'll hire some expert tutor

to torture me. He won't let me ride after school. He's *said* all this."

"Hey, we're getting out of here this weekend. He's letting you go on the trip, right? So don't even think about it." Laurie scooted closer to Patrick. "Okay? Come on, Patrick Fitzpatrick. Cheer up."

"Yeah, 'cause if you don't? Then we're all in trouble," I said.

But Patrick didn't laugh or smile. He wouldn't even look at me.

I just sat there and watched him and Laurie get closer and closer, like a door that was slowly being shut, with them on one side and me on the other.

CHAPTER SIXTEEN

"In from the sticks, huh?" Mr. Garcia's sister Anita smiled as she opened the door to her Back Bay town house apartment. She had long, dark brown hair, and was wearing a black V-neck sweater, jeans, and black boots with stiletto heels.

Mr. Garcia laughed and gave his sister a quick hug. "We got out on good behavior."

"Even you? Wow."

"Actually, I think we got out on bad behavior." Kelley looked at Patrick, then laughed. She'd somehow warmed to him on the van ride to Boston, or maybe she just automatically loosened up as soon as she left school grounds.

"Come on in, guys." Anita smiled at me as I walked through the door. "Hi."

"Hi." I stepped into the living room and made room for everyone else filing through the doorway behind me with their backpacks and duffel bags. Anita's apartment had hardwood floors, cool, patterned rugs, and a mixture of art prints on the walls.

It was a relief to get out of the van after our two-hour ride. With every mile we traveled, and every exit we passed, I'd started dreading getting here more and more. This was supposed to be the highlight of spring term. But instead of being excited like everyone else, my stomach hurt, and I felt carsick. In a way, I didn't want to come, but how could I get out of it? Besides, I wouldn't want to be stuck at home for the whole weekend. I'd only be leaving myself open to questions from Dad, from Mr. Garcia, from Kook if I didn't come.

It didn't help that I didn't have Laurie to lean on, to distract me. Things had definitely changed. She and Patrick were including me in everything, and at the same time it was like it didn't matter at all whether I was there or not. They kept making inside jokes to each other, referring to things I didn't know about.

In the van, Laurie had scooted over next to the window, Patrick sat in the middle, and I had the aisle. It was the way we sat in geometry class, reversed. It wasn't like geometry class though, because Patrick wasn't being funny and sweet to me or offering me candy or passing me notes. Instead, I had to sit there and watch as Patrick reached over to squeeze Laurie's knee and leaned against her. Serial flirt, I thought. Just like his dad. How could I be so stupid to think he actually cared about me, to think it mattered?

"Anita, this is everyone. Everyone, meet Anita." Mr. Garcia took off his black leather jacket and folded it across the back of a kitchen chair.

"You guys know he only arranges these school trips so he can stock up on new clothes," Anita said.

"Don't forget the restaurants," Mr. Garcia added, patting his slightly round belly.

"Hey, why do you think *we're* here?" Laurie said. "It's nice to meet you—I'm Laurie."

"This place is great," Patrick said, looking around the apartment.

"Thanks. Did you find a parking space okay?" Anita asked, closing the door behind Jason.

"Does the curb count?" Dave joked.

"A simple 'yes' would also work," Mr. Garcia said with a sigh.

"You girls can put your stuff upstairs in the guest room—there's a foldout sofa and a couple of air mattresses," Anita said. "And the guys will be down here—there's a futon in the office, and the couch is quite comfortable. So, what's your schedule for this conference again?"

"Tonight we're on our own," Mr. Garcia began.

"Tomorrow there are classes and seminars all day, and a dinner reception. Sunday we have breakfast and the awards ceremony," Kelley said.

"Then I thought we could hit some museums in the afternoon before we head home. And then we thought that we could stay an extra night or two, and maybe go back home on Tuesday," Laurie added.

"Or not," Patrick said. "We could always stick around for the entire week and write a special city edition."

Kelley shot him a look. "We've probably had enough special editions."

"Okay, everyone—why don't you put your stuff upstairs and unwind for a half hour or so. Then we can all head out for a walk, grab some dinner," Mr. Garcia said. "I'll pick Anita's brain for a restaurant recommendation."

"I'd better come to dinner with you, so you don't get lost," Anita said.

"That would be great. Can I hire you to be an extra chaperone for the weekend? Our other teacher fell through," Mr. Garcia started to explain as we walked up the circular stairs to the second floor of the town house.

"This is so cool. Isn't it?" Laurie asked.

"Yeah. Sure," I said and I tried to smile, to be enthusiastic like everyone else, but inside I felt sort of like a time bomb. We'd only been there a few minutes, but I was already ready to get out of there. The tension was building inside me, because I kept wondering where we would go to eat and worrying that I'd see something that reminded me of last time.

Everything already reminded me of last time. Seeing the skyline, going through traffic rotaries, passing a dozen Dunkin' Donuts shops, getting stuck in traffic, looking up at the Prudential, at the "T" signs, at the crowds of people walking down sidewalks. I shouldn't be here, I kept thinking. I'm not ready to be here.

• • •

We went to a Thai restaurant in Anita's neighborhood. I couldn't eat much, but I was relieved because I had never seen it before, had never been down that block. After dinner, I gave Kelley money for my meal, which I'd barely eaten, and went outside to wait for everyone while they settled the bill. It was snowing when I walked out the door, which was bizarre. Two days ago it had been warm and sunny—now it was thirty degrees and snowing. I was glad to be wearing my black fleece vest over my sweater—being cold all the time meant I was actually prepared for the change in weather.

Patrick was the first one out the door behind me. We exchanged awkward glances. I wondered if he'd come out after me because he wanted to talk.

"Weird, huh?" I said, trying to make conversation. I couldn't stand that he wasn't talking to me anymore, that he was acting like a polite acquaintance. Suddenly I hated being alone with him like this. It reminded me of how it used to be when it was just us, and how I could never really handle it. "It's not supposed to snow in April."

"Hm," he murmured, turning up the collar of his jean jacket.

"So did you get your Thai food fix?" I asked. "Remember that time you came to the bowling alley and pretended you thought Birch Bowl was a Thai place?"

He didn't say anything.

I moved over to stand closer to him under the awning. "Patrick? What's going on?"

Patrick looked at me. "You know exactly what's going on." His voice was cold when he said it, sort of unrecognizable. "You're the one who told me how it was supposed to be."

I couldn't think of anything else to say. He was right: He was only doing what I'd asked. But maybe I hadn't known what I was asking for when I said it. I'd wanted him to like Laurie the way she liked him. But now that he did, it was awful. They were together now. And yet he was still angry with me, almost as if he were doing this to spite me, which wasn't fair to Laurie, either.

We all walked around the neighborhood after dinner together, checking out stores and meandering around Copley Square. Laurie and Patrick had their arms around each other's shoulders, and I was walking behind them by myself, watching the giant snowflakes land on Laurie's old black leather jacket—the one she'd bought predistressed at Salvage City—and turn to water. She was wearing khaki capris and I wondered if her legs were cold, but I couldn't ask because she was too busy talking to Patrick, not to me. Kelley was of course up front with Anita and Mr. Garcia, and everyone else trailed behind them.

Laurie was laughing and trying to catch snowflakes on her tongue. "I can't believe it's snowing in April. This is so crazy!"

"And I thought Maine winters were long," Patrick joked.

"Oh, my god. The last time we were here it was so hot," Laurie said. "We usually come in June every year when school gets out, with our moms," she explained to Patrick. "But last year. Wow. It was so hot. Like ninety-eight or something."

"Don't talk about last year," I said quietly. Please don't talk about it.

"We all went out to eat, like we always did, but Alison's mom wasn't hungry—she hardly ate anything. And then we went outside and she just like . . . collapsed. Like she was really weak."

"Laurie, shut up," I said. I felt like I shouted it, but my voice came out as a whisper.

"We thought it was the heat, you know. But then my mom said no, it wasn't the heat. And then Alison's mom said she had to tell us something. She said she'd gone in for a bunch of tests recently. I mean, we didn't even know she went to the doctor—we had like *no* idea. So then she just like has us sit down on this park bench, sort of on the edge of the park, so there wouldn't be anyone around, and she tells us—"

"Shut up," I said again, a little louder this time.

Laurie stopped and turned around. "I'm telling Patrick what happened. It's not like it's not on your mind, too. I can tell, okay? I know that look you have, the one you get when you think about it. See, one of her rules is that she's never going to talk about it. Because then somehow that will mean it never happened," she said to Patrick.

"That's not why," I said angrily. I couldn't believe she was discussing this—at all. It was up to *me* to bring it up when I wanted to, and I didn't want to. She knew that. Did she feel like she could do it just because we weren't back home? Or because Patrick was there and she was acting closer to him now than to me?

"Like another rule? Is never using her locker," Laurie said, staring at me. "You know how your dad is always saying how we're attached at the hip? Well, we couldn't be, because that *bag* of yours is. I mean, I don't know how you can carry it. And you should be walking funny now, since you don't have it for once."

"You know, you shouldn't give her such a hard time. I mean, it's cool to carry a bag," Patrick said. "I have to think that, because of my courier bag—"

"At some point they're going to make her open her locker and then, wham!" Laurie went on. "All kinds of stuff is going to come flying out. Grade reports, notes for meetings she missed, love notes, Valentines, notes from Kook, Valentines from Kook—"

"Stop it!" I said. Why was she being so mean, why was she trying to hurt me? She thought she was being funny, but she wasn't. The second she brought up the last time, she stopped being funny. Even she didn't know, not really. She didn't know the reason I wouldn't use my locker was because I'd been standing at it when I was paged to the principal's office and my father was waiting there for me and I knew why the second I saw him and couldn't stand hearing the words and ran out the door and down the hall and slammed through the front exit and across the lawn with my father running after me, then stopping, then running again until he caught me.

"I mean, who knows what's in there, right? An entire colony of ants or cockroaches could be living inside," Laurie said. "It might be condemned."

"So what," I said. "Who cares."

"Hey, Laurie. Leave her alone. We should probably try to catch up to everyone else," Patrick said. "Come on, guys. Let's go."

But I didn't move, and neither did Laurie. I didn't understand why she was being so mean to me. She was standing there, criticizing me, making fun of me.

"Tell you what, Alison. Patrick and I will get you a new locker combination for your birthday. Would that help?" Laurie asked with a smile.

"Hey, give her a break. It takes some people longer to deal with stuff," Patrick said.

"Well, she's setting a record," Laurie said.

"What do you know?" I stared at them—smugly holding hands and the way they were standing so close. "What do you guys know about anything? You know, you're always criticizing your dad for being a serial flirt. But look at you.

It's only been a week since you told me you liked me. And now you're all over her."

"All over her?" Patrick stared at me and dropped Laurie's hand. "Why do you care, anyway? That's what you wanted, right?"

"Is that the only reason why you're doing it?" I said. "Just to get back at me?"

"What do you mean, that's what she wanted?" Laurie stared at Patrick. "What are you guys talking about?"

"It's ridiculous. You're both ridiculous," I said.

"Yeah, okay, whatever, Alison. You're not?" Patrick started to jog slowly ahead to catch up with Mr. Garcia and the rest of the group, now about a block ahead of us.

"What were you talking about—when did he tell you he liked you?" Laurie blinked a snowflake off her eyelashes. "He doesn't *like* you."

"You wouldn't even be with him now if it weren't for me," I said angrily. She wanted to hurt me; she had just humiliated me in front of Patrick. I could hurt her just as easily.

"What? I'm the one who got us to do stuff with him. Like I always am. I mean, leave it up to Laurie, as always." She threw up her hands.

"That's not what I mean."

She laughed. "Then what? What are you talking about?"

"He doesn't like you," I said. "Not really. He never liked

180

you, except as a friend. It was me."

She stared at me, her hair covered with snow, her eyes shining in the light from the streetlamp. "You're lying."

The snow was falling harder now—big, heavy, wet flakes that dissolved on impact, cool against my cheek. Suddenly I knew that I wasn't sticking around for the rest of this weekend. I would be gone tonight. I would get away from here, from last time, from Laurie. "I'm not lying," I said.

"You are. You're pissed at me, because for once in like, months, I asked you to talk about it, and so you're making something up to hurt me—"

"I'm not," I cut her off. "He came to see me, he told me how he felt. But I told him not to like me, to like you instead, because I knew how you felt. So you're together now. So you could thank me instead of attacking me."

Laurie shook her head. "No. That's crazy. Patrick and I hit it off from the beginning. We only hung around you because we *had* to, because you couldn't be alone—"

"No, that's not true. I saw him lots of times when you weren't there!" I protested. "You know what? *I* was the one who always said, let's call Laurie. Not Patrick. And I did it because I knew you'd want to be there."

"Right!" Laurie laughed. "The only reason you called me was because you couldn't handle it, you couldn't take being alone with him. Because you can't handle anything anymore."

Snowflakes were landing on my eyelids, my cheeks, and

clumping in my hair.

"I'm sorry," Laurie said. "I shouldn't have said that."

"No, you're right. I can't handle anything. I'm going home. Have a great weekend, okay? Have a really, really great time. Tell Mr. Garcia I'll be fine. I know where the bus station is. I can remember that, anyway," I said as I started walking away, toward the "T" station.

"Where's she going?" I heard Patrick call to Laurie, and I began to run. "Alison, where are you going?" he called. "Hey, Alison!"

"Leave her alone," Laurie said. "That's what she wants. That's all she ever wants!" she shouted after me.

CHAPTER SEVENTEEN

I sat in the very front seat on the bus, on the right side of the driver, watching the windshield wipers go back and forth, back and forth. It would make me cross-eyed if I had to drive and look into those. It was making me cross-eyed now, but there was something soothing about the rhythm of it. I was mesmerized by the fat white snowflakes being driven into the windshield as we left the city behind us and barreled down Route 2.

A woman with short gray hair, wearing a short-sleeved Hawaiian shirt, was sitting next to me. It didn't make sense that she was wearing a summer shirt in the snow, but there she was.

I knew about this bus because we'd taken it that one time a few years ago. Fortunately it ran a few times a day, and I got to the station just as one was about to leave—the evening run. Bringing people back home after a day of shopping in the city—or whatever they'd been doing.

I didn't know why I was in such a hurry to jump on the bus and head home. I'd hate it as soon as I got there.

"Aren't you cold, ma'am?" the bus driver asked the woman next to me, after we stopped to drop off several passengers in Concord. He sank into the driver's seat, the cushion whooshing under his weight, and closed the bus door.

"No. Oh, no. You've got the heat nice and warm. Besides, I didn't bring much of a jacket. I just got back from Tampa. Flew into Logan. My daughter's going to pick me up. Of course—snow. Who expects to come back to snow in April?" She turned to me. "What a strange day."

"Yeah," I agreed. "Very strange." That was an understatement.

"So, how about you?" She smiled. "Where are you coming from?"

"Oh—just Boston," I said.

"Just Boston? I'd say not. That's quite a trip." She shifted in the seat, wrapping her arms around herself.

"Do you want my vest?" I asked.

"Well . . . now that you mention it, I am a bit chilled. Are you sure?"

"Sure. I'm warm enough, so—go ahead." I handed her my fleece vest, and she tucked it around her shoulders like a blanket.

"Thank you. Now, are you all by yourself?"

"Well, I was with friends, but . . . " Now I don't have them anymore. "They wanted to stay longer, and I had to get home, so."

"Really? Is it all right for you to be traveling alone?"

"Oh, sure."

"Won't your mother worry?"

I couldn't say anything at first. I hated when this happened. I wanted her to drop it, but she was just sitting there, looking at me, waiting for my answer. "No," I said. "She won't."

"Really? I would be worried about you."

"Well, she's not around," I said. "I mean. It's just my father."

"They're divorced?"

I shook my head.

"Oh, I see. Well." She reached over and patted my knee. "That's a shame. That's awful. What happened?"

I just looked at her, then at the floor, and then at the windshield wipers and the snow whirling on the road ahead of us.

"I'm sorry. If you don't want to talk about it, that's fine," she said.

And as I was thinking, no, I don't want to talk about it, out of nowhere I heard my voice—I heard myself say, "Cancer," and then I was telling her. How it happened. How it came on so fast and yet seemed to take forever, how every day was made up of hours that seemed endless and yet short. How my mother hadn't checked herself. How she hadn't gone to the doctor in a few years because, well, why? She felt fine, or said she did. She and Laurie's mom used to joke about it, how they weren't going in for a checkup until a cute young male doctor came to Birch Falls to practice, or at least until "the Good Old Boy and the Bitch," the only family practice in town, left. The Good Old Boy was Dr. Calibri, Kevin's grandfather, and the Bitch was his office partner, Dr. Parzutti.

It didn't matter that we had great insurance because of Dad's job, that the entire visit would be almost free. It didn't matter that Dad pushed her to go or that the receptionist hinted she should schedule an appointment when she brought me and Sam in for our yearly checkups, so we could participate in school sports.

That day in the park she'd told us that by the time she actually went—when she noticed something weird going on with her body, when she realized that she wasn't feeling so great, that in fact she felt exhausted and weak and it wasn't because she was working long hours or getting older— she had aggressive-growth breast cancer that had already spread from her breast to her lymph nodes to her liver and was moving into her bones. To everywhere. She didn't have much time left, although they thought maybe . . . at first . . . something could be done. But as it turned out, it really couldn't.

She didn't say it, but I knew that day in the park: It was going to be our last trip to Boston together. That the mother-daughter party was almost over.

• • •

We were still talking about it when the bus pulled up at her stop. She was telling me a story that wasn't all that different, about one of her friends who hadn't made it, either, but who'd hung on for a year and a half. A year and a half. What would that be like? Would it be any different? I wondered. Would it better, or worse? Or just as equally bad?

"Oh! We're here!" she said. "There's my daughter." She pointed to a woman standing outside in the parking lot, wearing a large down coat. "I'm so glad I got a chance to talk with you. And don't worry." She unwrapped my vest from her shoulders and handed it to me. "Everything will turn out all right. . . . What's your name?"

"Alison."

"Well, Alison, I just feel like I have to give you a hug."

Don't hug me, nobody hugs me anymore, I wanted to say as she was already wrapping her arms around my shoulders. I felt a tickle in my throat. I hadn't let anyone hug me like that in a long time. Why was it a stranger on a bus wearing a Hawaiian shirt?

She stood up and carefully climbed down the bus steps, the driver helping her down the last one because the snow was making things slippery. He unloaded her suitcase, while she and her daughter greeted each other with a curt peck on the cheek.

I had planned on walking home from the bus stop, which was right in front of the gas station, but since it was still snowing when I got off the bus, I went inside and called a cab. I could use my leftover trip money to pay for it. The dispatcher said it would take a while for the cab to come, maybe twenty minutes, which was fine because I needed time to think about what I was going to say to my father when I got home. I'd tell him I wasn't feeling well—or that it turned out there wasn't enough room at Anita's after all. Whatever I said, I didn't want to get into any discussion about it. Not with him. Not now.

Maybe he wouldn't be home, I hoped.

I wished there was someone I could talk to about what had happened, but it wasn't him. He wouldn't know what to say and, for that matter, neither would I.

Anyway, it's wasn't just about Laurie and Patrick. It was about everything.

When the cab pulled up at our house, I paid the driver, got out, and walked up to the porch. I knew exactly how this would go. Dad and Sam would be hanging out, watching a movie. They'd be laughing and having fun, and eating pizza and candy, and they'd look up at me like I was a member of someone else's family, a distant cousin come to visit.

They'd be just back from a baseball game. Even in the snow, Sam would have hit a home run—at least one and probably more. He'd be having the day of his life.

And then there was me. We were such opposites. He was younger than I was, and he was dealing with everything better. It wasn't fair. He had Dad.

"Hello?" my dad's voice called as I closed the door behind me. "Alison, is that you?"

I walked through the front door and into the living room.

He was crouched on his knees, beside a half-filled cardboard box. "Alison! Oh, I'm so glad to see you. Is everything okay? Are you all right?"

"Sure. Of course I am." I stopped and stared at the box on the floor beside him. Her picture looked back at me. Her picture that used to be on top of the bookshelf. "Wh—what are you doing?" I asked.

Dad stood up. "Never mind that—what are *you* doing home from Boston?"

"Never mind?" I looked around the living room and noticed a few trash bags by the staircase. "What's all this?"

"Some clothes. I didn't think you'd want them—I mean, you went through and took what you wanted so . . . "

"What are you *doing*?" I asked.

"I thought I could get some things . . . cleared out over the weekend. Just to the garage—we can keep them until we decide what to do with them. . . . " Dad babbled.

I stared at the dark green garbage bags full of clothes. Cheap, flimsy, Salvage City, half-defective garbage bags that would fall apart as soon as he picked them up. "Don't!" I said. "Don't *do* that!"

I ran upstairs to my room and slammed the door behind me. I picked up books and folders from my desk and threw them across the room, onto the floor. I tore the last few photos off my bulletin board—I didn't want to look at pictures of Laurie anymore. I didn't want to look at anyone who was laughing or smiling or having a good time. I tossed my leather pen cup against the wall and smashed the cordless phone into the desk. I opened my dresser and started flinging my clothes out behind me. I didn't want any of this stuff. I wanted to get rid of all of it. If Dad could throw out everything that reminded him of her, then I could, too. And what didn't? My entire life was a reminder. My calendar. My clothes. My hair.

"Alison, stop! What are you doing?" Dad rushed into my room, even though the door was shut, even though he wasn't allowed to do that.

My arms were hanging at my sides, and I was out of breath. I picked up an old notebook and dropped it into the trash can. I couldn't look at him.

"Why are you home early?" he asked.

"I just felt like it."

"Come on. Talk to me. Is that the whole story?" Dad asked.

"What do you mean?" I said. "Of course it is."

"No. That isn't the whole story—that you just *felt* like leaving. Explain it to me, Alison. Talk to me. People don't just walk away from field trips. That isn't like you."

I couldn't say anything. How did he know what was *like* me and what wasn't?

"Mr. Garcia's called here three times already, worried about you," he said.

"He shouldn't worry. I told him I was going to be fine," I lied.

"Well, he obviously didn't believe you. And it's on his head if anything happens to you."

"So I'll call him and tell him I'm still fine," I said.

"Hey. I know you're upset, and I'm sorry you're feeling so bad. But don't take that tone with me," Dad said.

"Leave me alone," I said.

"No. I'm not going to leave you alone."

"Why not?" I said. "That's what you're good at."

My father grabbed both my arms. "I'm upset because you ran away from the trip. I was worried! Do you know what could have happened to you?"

"You should call Laurie's mom if you're worried. *She* might know where I was," I said. "She actually knows me, she actually cares about me—"

"And you think I don't? Do you think I ever think about anyone else but you and Sam and how all this is affecting you?"

This. We couldn't even say her name. She was a "this" now.

It was the first time we'd talked about her in a long time, and it was so wrong that this was the discussion. I didn't want to get into it with him. "Look, why don't you go back to pitching stuff?"

"That's not . . . I can do that later. I'm sorry. I don't know what I was thinking." He paused. "I thought that's . . . what you'd want." He looked around at my room now, at the bare walls, the empty bulletin board, the floor covered with clothes and papers and books. "Is it?"

"No," I said, not looking at him.

"Okay. Okay." He rubbed his finger against a black mark on the wall, where I'd thrown the pen holder. "You're going to come downstairs with me and call Mr. Garcia now, since it looks like this phone is out of order." He picked up the smashed cordless from the floor. "What did this phone ever do to you?"

He was trying to joke around and cheer me up, but it wouldn't work.

I went downstairs to the living room, tried to ignore the half-packed box on the floor, and picked up the phone. "Here's the number." Dad handed me a sheet of notepaper. "I think he's pretty much waiting by the phone." He sat on the sofa beside me so I couldn't get away with not calling. I didn't want to call. It was embarrassing, humiliating.

When Mr. Garcia answered and found out it was me, he let out a huge sigh of relief. "So you made it home all right. Thank God. When Laurie said you went to the bus station, I panicked—and by the time I got there, you were gone."

"I was lucky. There was a bus leaving almost right away," I said. "So, no problem. I got home safe and sound."

"Well, that's good to hear. Very good. But, Alison? What happened to you?" Mr. Garcia said.

I couldn't answer him. What could I say? My life fell apart, and I have no idea how to put it back together? You couldn't just *say* those things.

I started to try to tell him I was sick, that I had a bad cold, but I couldn't get the lie out. It just wasn't worth the effort. Mr. Garcia would know I was lying, anyway. I'd never once complained about feeling sick.

"Is everything okay?" Mr. Garcia asked. "I'm kind of worried about you."

"It's fine," I said. "I'm fine."

"Alison, I hate to interfere in kids' lives. You know that. I mean, half the time, you guys have way more figured out than I do, and you know it. But maybe you should think about talking to someone. Maybe Mr. Cucklowicz next week—I know you're trying really hard, and you're doing great. But sometimes . . . sometimes it's hard to get through something without a little help. You know what I mean?"

Now even Mr. Garcia, the only teacher I really liked, was ganging up on me. But my father was sitting next to me on the sofa and I could never confide in Mr. Garcia when he was there. "Yeah. Sure," I said.

"We miss you," Mr. Garcia said. "Hey, would you like to talk to Laurie? She's right here."

"N-no," I said. "No thanks."

"We'll tell you everything that happens—all the gory details—when we meet on Monday."

Monday. I couldn't think about Monday now. To get to Monday I'd have to get through Saturday, then Sunday. And I just didn't want to play this game anymore.

After I hung up the phone, I went back upstairs to my bedroom, picked my way across the cluttered floor to my bed, climbed in, and pulled the covers over my head.

CHAPTER EIGHTEEN

Dad knocked on my bedroom door at about one o'clock on Sunday afternoon. "Alison? We're going bowling," he said.

"Okay. Have fun," I said, not looking up from my biology textbook.

"Have fun? What are you talking about? You're coming," he said, stepping into my room.

I shook my head. "No, I'm not. I'm not going. I have too much homework to do." That was another lie but a harmless one, I thought. I didn't want to leave the house.

"Well, look. I'm not leaving you here by yourself," he said.

I turned around and looked up at him. "Why not?"

"I'm just not. You're coming, and you can either bowl or you can watch us or you can play pinball, I don't care. But this is a family outing and that means we all go. Five minutes, okay?"

Family outing. I wanted to throw something at the door when he closed it.

As we rode to the bowling alley, I sat in the backseat

and stared out the window. The spring snowstorm had passed and today was in the fifties, so the snow was melting quickly. Sam and Dad were going on and on about some upcoming baseball game, and how the pitcher had a reputation for being impossible to get hits off, how they'd been studying tapes of his technique. It was unbelievable to me how they could have the stupidest conversations, how they could talk and talk about nothing.

They had no idea what I'd been through, what I was going through. They didn't know Laurie and I were no longer attached at the hip and we probably wouldn't be again. In a way, all morning, I kept expecting her to call me from Boston. But of course she didn't.

The whole situation was impossible. She was in Boston, and I wasn't. She was with Patrick, and I wasn't.

Or maybe she and Patrick weren't together. I wondered how things were between them now. Had I ruined it for her? I wondered, and felt bad. But then I remembered the things she'd said, how she'd cut me down in front of Patrick, how she'd made me seem so pathetic, and I hoped she wasn't happy, either.

Dad took a detour on the way to Birch Bowl. "We're out of Mister Fizzee," he said as he pulled into the Salvage City parking lot.

Are you sure it's not cheap trash bags? I wanted to say. Are you sure you don't need another box of those?

But I'd noticed they were gone, and they weren't in the

garage, either, so maybe he had put everything back into the bedroom closet. But I wouldn't ask about it.

I got out of the car, and we all walked up to the front door. There was a yellow piece of paper posted on the door, and written in red ink were the words CLOSED FOR INVENTORY.

"How bizarre," my dad said. "Since when do they take inventory?"

"What's inventory?" Sam asked.

"That's when you tally up every item you have, so you know the total value of your stock. Businesses have to do it for tax purposes. Of course, most of them don't do it in the middle of the month, but . . . " He shrugged. "Oh well. I'll drop by tomorrow."

"You know what would be funny? If sometime we came here and they were closed due to a fire." Sam said. "Or like, there'd be this sign on the door. CLOSED: BROKEN PIPE. WATER DAMAGE. Get it? Get it?" He looked at me eagerly for a reaction.

"Yeah. Really funny," I said, getting back into the car. "Hilarious."

Sam glanced at me over his shoulder as he slid into the front seat. "Your sense of humor sucks. Has anyone ever told you that?"

Birch Bowl was almost empty, but Rick assigned us to a lane right next to some people in lane 10, right in the middle, even though we were the only other people there. I was about to request another lane, but then I realized how much I really didn't care.

"Size seven," Rick said, pushing a pair of familiar-looking shoes toward me.

I didn't even bother to tell him, "No, Rick, I take a size eight," again. I didn't care if the shoes didn't fit. I could just wear my socks, like we used to when we were little. I wasn't going to play anyway, so what did it matter?

"She's an eight," Sam said. He took the shoes out of my hands and handed them back across the counter. "Aren't you? She's definitely an eight."

"Oh. Sorry." Rick quickly replaced the shoes.

"Well, some people would say a perfect ten, actually," Dad joked. He was still trying to cheer me up from Friday night, and it still wasn't working.

Sam handed the shoes to me. "Why didn't you say anything?"

Because I don't care, I thought, but I didn't want to be mean so I just didn't open my mouth. We walked down to lane 9, and of course Dad somehow knew the people in 10, like he always did, because at some point he'd sold one of them, or all of them, insurance. So he was off and running, making small talk again.

I just sat in one of the seats behind the scoring table. I slipped off my shoes and put the bowling shoes on. When I was done, Sam was already finished bowling his first frame. Dad was still chatting with the men next to us. I just stared at them for a minute, wondering who they were and what they were laughing about. I couldn't stop thinking about Boston, about what everyone would be doing right now. Laurie would have accepted some award, Kelley would have pouted over not receiving one, and now they'd be off to the science museum, the Museum of Fine Arts, or the aquarium.

"Come on, Alison. Your turn." Sam was standing in front of me, tapping the end of my shoes with his toes.

"You go again. I don't want to," I said.

"Sure you do," Sam said.

"I didn't want to come," I said. "Dad made me."

"I don't care. It's only good if the three of us do it. I'm not just playing against Dad."

"What does it matter whether I play?"

"It's what we do," Sam said. "That's what we do on Sundays."

"No," I said.

Sam stepped up, grabbed a bowling ball off the rack, and came back toward me. He shoved the bowling ball into my hands, and it jammed against the end of my fingers. He was acting so strangely, as if we were little kids again and we were wrestling on the living room carpet. Now the people in lane 10 with Dad were watching us—Dad was watching us.

"It's your turn," Sam said. "Take it."

I let the ball roll off my fingers and drop to the floor.

"Pick it up." Sam was glaring at me. "You know what?" he said. "I hate you sometimes. I really, really hate you." He ran up to the front door and went outside. The alley was so quiet that I could hear the little bell over the door jingle as he opened it and went out.

My father hurried over to me. "Alison, what was that all about?"

I didn't say anything. I didn't know what it was about.

"Your brother seemed upset. Do you think you could try to think about his feelings sometimes?" He started to move toward the door, but I jumped up and grabbed his elbow.

"Don't. I'll go," I said.

When I went out front, Sam was making snowballs that were half snow and half mud and pitching them against the trees at the edge of the parking lot.

"Sorry," I said.

He didn't turn around. He wouldn't look at me. He just kept molding snow-mud balls.

"Sam, I'm sorry," I said. "I'm being a jerk."

He fired a snow-mud ball against the concrete wall of the car wash next door, and it splattered into pieces. He really had a good arm. "Just because you got kicked off your field trip and have to actually spend the weekend with us—"

"I didn't get kicked off. I left," I said.

"Whatever," Sam said. "Why did you leave?"

There was snow melting and dripping off the roof onto my neck, so I moved a few steps closer to him. "Because. I had a huge fight with Laurie."

"You and *Laurie* fought? What about?"

I picked up a chunk of slush and molded it into a ball. "Everything." I hurled the chunk toward a tree, but the slushy snow broke apart in midair.

"Everything what?" Sam asked.

I didn't want to explain, but I owed him something. "How . . . you know. How life sucks."

He looked at me and shrugged. "Yeah. What else?"

"How. You know. How I don't want to do some things . . . or talk about some things."

Sam didn't respond, which was really good of him. He could have jumped all over me then, about being "so not fun," if he wanted to.

"And we got in a fight about Patrick," I added. I didn't know why I was telling him all this; I guess because he liked Patrick.

"What about Patrick?"

"He and Laurie started going out—"

"But he likes you. He's always hanging around you," Sam said. "I don't get it."

"Yeah." I sighed. "There's a lot I don't get."

Sam perched on the hood of our car and tilted his face

toward the sun. "Why did you really leave the trip?"

"I don't know," I said. But that wasn't true. "I—I started thinking about stuff I didn't want to think about. Because. Laurie started talking about, you know. The last time we were there. And what happened."

"What happened?" Sam asked gently.

I wanted to tell him exactly how it had been. I really, really wanted to be able to. "It's just . . . Mom wasn't feeling all that great. And it showed. So it was when she had to tell me that she was sick. That she'd be starting chemo soon."

"Oh. Yeah, I remember that day," Sam said. "I mean, when she told me."

"Where? Was Dad there, too?" I asked.

He shook his head. "You know how you guys always went to Boston and that was like your thing? Well, she always took me to Jerry's. Usually on Wednesdays, after school—when she'd get out a little early and if I didn't have practice or something. To play pinball. She was good, you know. She taught me."

"Really?" I laughed. "I never knew that."

"Yeah, well. She said I shouldn't tell Dad, that he'd get mad at us for spending money on pinball and pizza." Sam jumped off the car hood and packed a snowball in his hands. "That's when she told me. On a Wednesday. Right when summer vacation started. She made it sound like no big deal, like it would all be fixed by the end of the summer.

You know? I was really mad at her about that."

I nodded. "Me, too. I hated that part. I hated that I was so . . . hopeful sometimes."

There was a jingling bell, and I glanced over at the door, expecting to see Dad coming out looking for us, and I kind of wished that he wouldn't.

Instead it was Rick standing at the door, holding it open. "You kids are ruining those shoes by getting them wet. If you stay out there any longer, you're going to have to pay for them."

"Dad will not let that happen," Sam said. He tossed the last snowball toward the street and we ran inside. We started furiously wiping the bowling shoe soles on the carpet. I knew we must look ridiculous. We started laughing hysterically, and then Sam said, "Speed bowling," and we shoved each other and sprinted back over to our lane.

CHAPTER NINETEEN

I found my duffel bag on the porch Monday morning. Someone—probably either Mr. Garcia or Laurie—had dropped it off but hadn't bothered to ring the doorbell. They must have gotten back late Sunday night. Or if it had been Laurie, then she didn't want to see me or talk to me. When I opened it up, I half expected there to be a note inside from her or Patrick or Mr. Garcia, or maybe a copy of the conference program or a ticket stub or *something*. But it was just my change of clothes and the other things I'd brought for the weekend.

It wasn't easy to avoid Laurie that day at school or any of the following days. In geometry class, she didn't talk to me, and I didn't see her talk to Patrick, either. None of us was on speaking terms. I didn't even look their way because I couldn't deal with making eye contact. It was too uncomfortable. It reminded me of little, stupid fights we'd had when we were younger, back in junior high. The silent treatment.

Laurie answered all of Mr. Lewis's questions and went

to the board and was brilliant and witty to everyone but cold to me. At lunchtime, I sat outside and ate by myself. Sometimes I brought lunch, and sometimes I didn't. I spent more time in the school library, doing homework, or sitting and staring at the wall.

Mr. Garcia found me there on Tuesday and asked why I hadn't come to journalism class, why I'd skipped the *Bugle* meeting, and left the trip. I kept it vague and told him I was having trouble keeping up with my other school-work, that I needed to cut down on other activities and focus. I didn't know if he bought it, but he left me alone after that.

I didn't go to school at all on Wednesday. So when I walked in on Thursday, Kook was waiting for me. "You're excused from your first class, Alison," he said. "Come with me."

"What's going on?" I asked.

"We need to talk. Where were you yesterday?" Kook said as we went into his office.

"I was home," I said. "I didn't feel well. Just a cold, I guess."

"And are you feeling better?" Kook asked.

"Yes. I feel . . . fine," I said slowly. What was he up to? What had I done wrong? Other people took sick days for a lot stupider reasons than I had.

"Would you like a muffin?" Kook offered.

"What?"

"They're low carb. My wife made them this morning." Kook opened a plastic container and held it toward me. "Go ahead. Take one."

I wasn't hungry at all, but I didn't feel like being psychoanalyzed for *not* having one, so I took one and had a small bite. I chewed it slowly. It didn't taste like anything to me. "I guess I'm not all better yet," I said. "My stomach." I put the nibbled muffin back on its wrapper on his desk.

"Alison. Have you heard the phrase 'going through the motions'?" Kook said.

"I guess. What does it mean?" I asked.

"You're just pretending. You're going to school every day—" He stopped to clear his throat. "Well, nearly every day. But you're not really. You don't talk in class—you don't talk to anyone except a few people."

"What's wrong with that? Everyone does that," I said. "They're called friends." Or they were, anyway.

"I feel like you're cutting yourself off from life," Kook said. "You were working on the paper, but you left during the school trip, and now you've quit. I mean, Alison, I'd rather have you involved and in trouble, like you were two weeks ago, than just doing nothing."

I didn't know what to say to that. I wasn't going back to the newspaper, though. It would be too embarrassing to be there with everyone after the way I'd behaved, running off as if I couldn't be away from home for a weekend.

"All right. I want you to sit here for five more minutes and write a list of things you care about—goals you have for the future. Then we can work on making plans of action to reach them." He handed me a notepad and a pen, then made himself busy looking through someone else's file.

I stared at the wall for a minute, at his diplomas. Why did he need to put so many up there? I wondered. It was like he was bragging, or he had something to show all of us so we wouldn't underestimate him and think he was just a wrestler.

I started writing a list of words that looked the same but sounded different. I knew there was a name for that, but I'd forgotten it.

"Kook, book, cook, kookbook, cookbook"

Then I skipped down a ways and wrote "GOALS" and "THINGS I CARE ABOUT."

There wasn't anything I could think of. I didn't have any big long-range goals.

"GOALS: To make it through the next week."

I thought about seeing Patrick that day on the bridge when I'd said that, how close I'd felt to him. All that was gone now.

"THINGS I CARE ABOUT: Sam. Laurie. Patrick."

"Well? How's it going?" Kook asked.

"I don't have anything yet." I tore out the sheet of paper and crumpled it into a ball.

"But I saw you writing," Kook said.

I shrugged.

"Alison, I would like to help you. That's all. Just an hour of your time, once a week."

I didn't say anything.

"Think about it, okay? Please?"

"Sure." I lifted my bag off the floor.

When I walked out of Kook's office at the end of the period, Kevin, Ryan, and Paul were standing right there in the hallway outside the door, talking. They glanced at me and then looked away, just like they always used to, back when I was a freshman, like they didn't really want anything to do with me.

Why did Kook's office have to be so centrally located, so visible? You had to advertise that you were having trouble to the entire school.

I was heading down toward the library when Ryan jogged up beside me. "Alison, haven't seen you around lately. Where have you been?"

"Nowhere," I said.

"What are you doing this weekend?" he asked.

"Nothing," I said.

"You should come down to the launch tomorrow night. There's going to be a big party—mostly seniors, but you could come. And a bunch of us are talking about going to the bridge," Ryan said. "You and Kuzmuskus should come," he said. "It'll be like . . . old times or something. I don't know." He laughed.

When I didn't respond, he walked in front of me, blocking my way into the library. "You look different," he said. "You're okay, right?"

"Sure," I said. "I'm fine."

He watched me for a few seconds, as if he were trying to decide if this was true. "Where's Kuzmuskus?" he asked. "I never see one of you guys without the other."

"We have different schedules," I said. "Come on, move. I have to write a paper by twelve. Get out of the way."

As I pushed past him into the library, he looked almost hurt that I didn't want to talk to him about why I was in Kook's office, that I didn't want to confide in him. As if I ever had.

"Home on Friday night? I must be seeing things." Dad rubbed his eyes and then squinted at me.

"Don't give her a hard time," Sam said from the living room floor, where he was stretched out, his head on a pillow. "She might bolt."

"Shut up," I said to him.

"Hey—hey. Don't talk to your brother like that. Where's Laurie?" Dad asked.

"I'm not sure," I said. I was getting really tired of that question.

He stared at me for a second, as if he knew something was up but he didn't know whether he was allowed to ask about it or not. "Well, we got one of those take-and-bake pizzas, and some movies. Why don't you pick the first flick?"

The three of us were just getting settled on the sofa when there was a knock at the door.

"Hey! I knew something was missing," Dad joked as he opened the door for Laurie. She usually just walked in, so this was weird. "What's with the knock?"

"Oh, you know. Trying to be formal," she said. "These sneakers are kind of working against me, though." She pointed to her worn-out, faded suede Vans.

"Well, come on in." Dad stepped back, and Laurie walked into the living room. I was so glad to see her. If she was coming here, that meant she was ready to apologize. Whenever we fought, she was the one who always came over first.

"Hey. Can we go upstairs?" she asked.

"Sure," I said.

"I knew they would ditch us," Sam said as he restarted the movie.

We went upstairs and into my room. I didn't know what to expect. We'd never had such a big fight before. How did you take back things you couldn't believe you'd said? How did you just move on from that? I had no idea where to start.

"So. Ryan invited us—both of us—to the launch tonight. Some senior party," I said.

"Mm. Yeah. I heard about it," Laurie said.

"Want to go?" I asked.

"No," she laughed. "Not really."

"Yeah. That's what I thought you'd say." I closed the door so that we could talk in private. Knowing Sam, he'd be up here to eavesdrop. He'd pretend he was coming upstairs to get something but really he'd just want to know what was up. "What, um . . . what made you come over?" I asked. "Tonight, I mean."

She took a deep breath before speaking. "So look, Alison. I've been thinking about it. You know. About the fight. Like, what it was really about. Why you freaked out, and why I kind of lost it and said all those things."

I sat down on my bed and looked at her. Why was she still criticizing me? "You were horrible about it. You were like taunting me or something."

"I know. And I'm sorry about that part. I guess." She picked at a piece of Scotch tape that was still stuck to the wall, pulling and pulling until the last tiny bit came off, bringing paint with it. "But in a way? I'm not."

"You're not?" That surprised me—and bothered me, too.

"No. Because—look. I had to say them. I've been wanting to say them. Because I've been with you like every single day for the last year and I've tried so hard to do everything the way you want, even when I think it's wrong. Or that *you're* wrong. I mean, what I said about not trying? You're not."

"Laurie?" I felt myself getting angry with her again, and tried to control my voice, to not yell. "You have no idea. It's different for you. You can deal with things. It's easy for you."

"Easy?" You think it's easy for me?" she scoffed.

I shrugged. "Yeah."

"Oh, sure. It's real easy. Hardly anything ever happens to me. Easy. Easy? Right." She walked over to the windows and looked out at the backyard. "You're so twisted the way you think sometimes. Like you're the only one who's ever had to deal with anything. I was friends with your mom. She was like . . . my aunt. And, Alison, my father is gone. *Gone*. He writes to me like once a year, or I get a card from his new wife and she signs his name. He doesn't want to have anything to do with me. And you have Sam. I don't have any brothers or sisters. Have you noticed? And then there's my mom. My mom, she's great. When she's around. Then she goes out partying and wakes up hungover and I'm the one who takes care of *her*. Okay?"

"So at least you get to do that," I said.

"True. And, yeah, you had a really crappy thing happen. It's like the worst thing. I don't know how that would feel, except I know that I miss her, too," Laurie said. "And so does my mom. But you won't even talk about it," she said. "About her."

"What is there to talk about?" I asked.

"Everything! The good stuff, the bad stuff . . . the

totally inconsequential stuff. I don't know. Look, I love you like you're my sister or something. But how are you ever going to get over it if you don't even try?"

I couldn't believe Laurie could ask that, couldn't believe she didn't *see*. Every day I got up and out of bed, I was trying. "I try," I said quietly.

"But you're not trying. And you know what? You can't walk around like this, you can't spend your life coming up with reasons you can't do things. Because you're so afraid, because you're worried you'll remember. You know, there's nothing *wrong* with remembering," Laurie said.

I sat there and stared at my bulletin board, thinking about the pictures that used to cover it. Me and Laurie in our goofy first-grade class photo. Swimming at King's Pond. Me holding Sam when he was a little baby, when they first came home from the hospital. The four of us in Boston Garden, perched on the duckling sculptures. And I remembered that feeling, that day last June, when I felt like someone had suddenly turned the park upside down and everything was spinning around me and I wanted to run but I couldn't, because it wouldn't help, it wouldn't make a difference, the same horrible thing would still happen. "Yes, there is," I said. "You don't know."

"No, I *do* know. It hurts. But shouldn't it? Isn't that the point?" She turned away from the window and faced me. "I mean, look. All I do is what you want. I don't make things hard for you. I let you get away with acting like you're not

213

even here half the time. I don't talk about things you don't want to talk about. At first that made sense. I could understand. But I can't do that forever, and neither can you. All I've been doing is thinking about what will make things easier for you. And I'm sick of it. I'm not going to do it anymore."

"I'm sorry," I said. "I'm sorry I'm not getting over it as fast as you are, that I'm too slow, that I'm not on the same timetable as everyone else—"

"Don't apologize!" Laurie said. "Just—don't. Look, I have to go. I can't stand here and argue with you about this—it's just . . . you can't, Alison. You can't stay like this." Her hand was on the doorknob, and she was about to leave. Then she turned around. "And you know what else? I don't want your leftover guys anymore. I don't want you and Patrick to feel sorry for me and set up some pity date—"

"That wasn't what it was like. I just told him—"

"No." She shook her head. "I don't want to hear it. It's really embarrassing. It's humiliating, actually. That you said no, I'm not interested, but how about my best friend, she likes you." Tears were running down Laurie's face. "I will find someone who likes me. On my own. And I really don't care what the two of you do. Run off together. Get married. Whatever. I'm not going to be the one who constantly tries to make you feel better while I feel worse and worse. Did you ever think *I* might need to forget stuff now and then? That I could use someone looking out for me?"

"I do look out for you," I said. "That's why I told Patrick I could never like him, because of you."

"But you were too late, weren't you? You already liked him. And vice versa. There wasn't really any room left for me. But, hey, I'm used to that." She opened the door.

"Where are you going?" I asked. We weren't finished, we hadn't made up yet. I didn't still want us to be fighting with each other—one week was more than enough.

"I don't know. Out," she said. "Anywhere but here. Look at your room. It's sad, Alison. It's pathetic. You used to have cool posters and that wall of pictures that you built up since like the sixth grade. I mean, if you're not going to use that bulletin board anymore, take it down. Throw out the pushpins. Put up a calendar or something." She closed the door behind her and I heard her sneakers clomping down the stairs.

The house was quiet, it was too quiet. I didn't want to think.

I opened my desk drawer and took out the disco CD Patrick had given me. I hadn't even listened to it yet. I put it into my CD player and pressed Play. I lay down on my bed and listened to the first song and thought about the three of us dancing in Patrick's barn, about Patrick getting slugged by Ryan, and the three of us sitting on the porch and Patrick leaning against me and me leaning away because Laurie was there.

Halfway through the third song, the CD started to skip. It made me want to cry, but I couldn't. I just stared at the ceiling and listened to the disc spinning around and the little laser eye trying to read it and failing.

I woke up when the phone rang in the hallway. I looked at my alarm clock, and it was 1:00 A.M. I couldn't imagine who it could be. A wrong number, probably.

I was annoyed that the phone had woken me up, and all I could think was, Please don't be Ryan calling drunk again. Please don't be Ryan calling and asking why I'm not at the launch.

I heard my father's low voice in the hallway, coming closer as he walked with the phone, and then going away, but I couldn't hear what he was saying.

"Alison?" Dad knocked on my door a few seconds later, just as I was drifting back to sleep. Before I could move, he walked in, turned on the overhead light, and came over to me. "Alison. That was Mrs. Kuzmuskus," he said softly, as if he were trying not to wake up Sam.

I jumped up in bed. "What's wrong?"

"Laurie—she's in the hospital. We need to get down there right away."

"What happened?" I looked at Dad and he was already dressed in jeans and a sweatshirt, his sneakers untied.

"She was with some guys, down at the launch. They went down to the bridge and jumped. Laurie didn't . . . " His voice cracked.

216

I couldn't ask him to finish the sentence, I didn't want him to. I couldn't talk, I couldn't breathe.

He reached out for my hands, to pull me up out of bed. I was shaking all over. "Alison, come on, get dressed and we'll go. We've got to hurry. Everything will be okay."

After he went out, I didn't know how I was moving around my room, putting on clothes, how I could take so long to figure out where my shoes were, how I was even still conscious of the fact I needed a baseball cap to cover up my slept-on hair, as if it mattered what I looked like, as if anything mattered.

I was stalling. I couldn't go back there.

CHAPTER TWENTY

We got to the hospital and found Mrs. Kuzmuskus pacing in the hallway, an unlit cigarette in her hand. She was wearing a large T-shirt and flannel pajama bottoms. When she looked at me, her eyes were flat, unexpressive. She didn't have her makeup on and she looked naked without it.

Then suddenly it was as if she realized it was me standing there, in the doorway, keeping the automatic doors wide open, unable to move further into the hospital, and her eyes widened, and tears started streaming down her face.

I wanted to run and hug her, but I was afraid to. I couldn't believe what was happening. This couldn't be happening. The three of us weren't here *again*.

And why was I so surprised, so caught off guard? I shouldn't have been. I should have started expecting the worst, because it always happened.

Dad moved awkwardly toward her, and she took a few steps toward us. They moved closer and closer until finally Dad clapped her on the shoulder and then wrapped his arms around her. I should go over there, I told myself. I should hug her, too. But I couldn't move. It was like my legs were frozen to the colored lines on the floor. I remembered my mother joking about them the first time she went in for tests. "They picked spumoni colors," she said. "Why do they want us to think about spumoni at the hospital?" And she was joking all the way through that first week and then suddenly there wasn't anything to joke about and only Dad kept trying, occasionally.

I wrapped my arms across my chest, because I was shaking all over. I hadn't been able to stop on the way here and now that I was here it was getting worse. I felt as if I'd stayed out too long in cold weather, like the time when Sam and I were little and we went sledding without mittens and nearly got frostbite. I tried to slow my breathing, to get myself under control.

"We're here, Jody," I heard my father say to Mrs. K. "What can we do?"

"Nothing," she said. "Nobody can do anything."

"I'm so sorry—"

"They were trying, but then . . . they said . . . no. Now they say I have to make arrangements. Arrangements. I mean, what am I supposed to do, who am I supposed to call? Do they think—"

"I'll take care of it, Jody," my father said.

And I knew that he would, that he would be good at that, because he probably knew the number already.

"My parents—Roger—"

"I'll call them," my father said. "Put it out of your mind."

I was watching them and I could hear them talking, but it was like I was standing behind a glass partition, like I was there with them and not there. Their voices were muffled. Besides us, in the emergency room waiting area, was a pregnant woman and her husband and their two young kids. A man dressed in black leather motorcycle gear was holding a blood-soaked towel to the side of his face. It was a typical Friday night shift for the regional hospital. Car accidents, baby deliveries.

But I wasn't ever here for anything typical. I wanted to be. So badly. Just once in my life I wanted to come here because Sam broke his arm or Dad had a fender bender or I sprained my ankle or had the flu or anything. Anything but this.

I walked up to Mrs. Kuzmuskus and put my hand on her arm. I don't know how I found the strength to say it. "Where is she?" I asked. "What room?"

"Alison . . . oh, god, Alison." She collapsed on my shoulder and started to sob.

I stood in the hallway outside the room where Laurie was, waiting to go in. Mrs. K. had just come out and it was my turn. My father stood behind me, as if he were waiting for me to make the first move, to do the hard part.

The last time I'd been at the hospital, I'd stood in the

hallway by myself while Sam and Dad were in the room, and I'd eaten an ice cream sandwich, which is what I did every time I came to visit my mother. I could make them last a long time. I would lick around the edges until the sandwich got flatter and flatter and then I would nibble at the chocolate cookie part. I did this because I wanted to stay out in the hallway as long as I could, because if I went into her room I couldn't ignore the facts. That she looked terrible. That she wasn't going to make it.

Which was obvious and I hated how obvious it was, because if I could see it, everyone in the room could see it and yet they were pretending it wasn't so bad, pretending there was hope.

I'd hoped at the beginning, which was the wrong thing to do. I'd never let myself hope again.

A nurse in yellow scrubs came up to me now as I stood outside the exam room. "Are you family?" she asked.

I nodded. "Yeah." I didn't really think about it, or whether that was lying or not, because it was the answer I was used to giving.

"Go in, it's okay," the nurse said, patting my shoulder.

I just stared at her. *It's okay.* People always said the worst, weirdest things when everything was a complete and utter disaster. Like "Nice day, isn't it?" when saying hello to the intensive-care nurses, or "good morning" or "thanks for coming" at a memorial service. And "I'm sorry." As if that would help.

I gently pushed the door open and went into the room.

Dad came into the room behind me, keeping his hand on the small of my back, as if I would faint and he would keep me from falling.

Laurie was lying there on the bed, next to the gurney they must have brought her in on. Her hair was hanging over the end, and when I walked up to the bed my foot slipped in a pool of water on the floor from where it was dripping. It didn't make sense that she could be dead and her hair could still be doing something.

I looked down at her face, at her clothes, the faded Captain Jack's T-shirt she'd worn in the *Bungle* picture. She was barefoot and her toenails were painted; her favorite color was shocking pink, but she'd alternated it now with white and bright red.

"Oh, god. Sam. I forgot *Sam*." And all of a sudden Dad was running out of the room to use the phone to call home.

At first I thought he had truly forgotten, that it was an honest mistake, but then I thought, no. He needed an escape. He wanted to get out of here; he needed to.

I thought about how he'd have to tell Sam what happened. How he was probably getting really tired of telling us horrible things, delivering the worst news imaginable. And I started worrying about my dad. And Sam. How he would react.

I took a deep breath and forced myself to look at Laurie's face. It was her, but it couldn't be her. Lying there. It couldn't be.

I knew that I should say something important. I knew that I was supposed to tell her good-bye, but I didn't know what to say, how to do this. I'd never known. I just stood there for a few minutes, looking at her, then looking at the wall, then her again. There were so many things to say, so many things to choose from—how could I pick the right one? But there was no right one. I could stay in here and talk all night, and it wouldn't be enough.

I touched Laurie's wrist, and then her arm. Her skin was cold. She was freezing cold. Laurie, the one who was always too warm. I leaned down and put my arms around her shoulders and then I hugged her, my cheek, my shirt, getting wet from her sopping, river-soaked clothes.

"Laurie," I said. "Laurie, don't jump. Laurie. Wait for me."

And I closed my eyes and hugged her tightly and pictured the two of us spray painting our initials and I could see Laurie instead insisting on writing out her full last name and then we were jumping off the bridge like we were supposed to when we were seniors.

When I walked back out into in the waiting room, both my father and Mrs. K. were surrounded by hospital people, making plans. A policewoman was there, interrogating the Gods, who wore wet shirts and jeans and shorts. The Gods. The Gods must have brought her in, I realized. They must have been here when we arrived, but I never even saw them.

I knew everyone was looking at me and wondering how I got so wet and assuming it was tears.

"How could you do this? How could you let this happen?" my father was asking Ryan and Kevin.

"Were you drunk?" I said.

"What?" Ryan asked. "No. Alison, I *swear*. We weren't drinking, we weren't."

"You drink?" My father was livid, looking as if he wanted to hit Ryan, to hit anyone within arm's reach.

"I told her not to do it," Kevin said. "I told her it was crazy—she wasn't ready—you can't jump at night the first time you do it."

I just watched him walk closer and closer to me, with this pleading look in his eyes.

"Get out of here!" my father said, pushing him back, shoving him toward the door.

"I know, it's my fault," Kevin said, his voice breaking.

"No, it's not," I said. "Laurie always does what she wants. She's not afraid of anything."

And then I was running out the door, running as fast as I could, getting as far away from that hospital as I could.

CHAPTER TWENTY-ONE

I don't know how I made it through the rest of the night and the next day. Ryan called; Patrick called; everyone called. People wanted to come over. My dad answered the phone every time, and told people I wasn't ready to see anyone.

My dad wouldn't let me go anywhere without him. He didn't ask how I was doing—he just never left a room while I was in it. Sam and I watched TV endlessly without speaking to each other, without talking at all. It was just like the time before. I kept waiting to completely break down and cry, but I couldn't.

Finally, on Sunday, Dad and Sam ran out to check on Mrs. Kuzmuskus and get some takeout food for her and us. "We'll be back in half an hour," Dad said. "Don't move from this spot."

I was sitting on the porch, reading, when a green pickup truck pulled up in front of the house. It was almost like he'd been around the corner, waiting until Dad left.

Ryan got out of the pickup and brushed off his jeans. "Hey. Do you have a minute?"

"Not really," I said.

"Alison, please. You've got to listen," Ryan said, stepping up onto the porch.

"No. I don't."

"How about . . . let's go for a walk or something," Ryan suggested.

I shook my head.

"Okay. Well, can I get something to drink? It's so hot."

I couldn't believe he wasn't leaving. What did he think, that I wanted to talk to him? But I didn't have the energy to tell him to leave. "Help yourself." I pointed to the door. "Kitchen is to the left."

"Yeah, okay." He went inside and came back with two cans of diet Mister Fizzee from Salvage City. "This is funny. You guys drink this crap, too? I thought only my family—" He stopped as he stood in front of me. "I didn't mean. Sorry. It's not funny. It's not crap."

"No, you're right. It's not very good." I took the can from him and cracked it open. There was a small hiss, as if this one actually had carbonation.

"So how are you doing?" Ryan asked.

I didn't say anything. What could I say?

"I asked Kevin and Paul to come with me today. But they couldn't. Or I guess, they didn't." Ryan tapped his fingers against the soda can. "They feel so bad, Alison. You know that. Don't you?"

"No. Not really." I took a sip of the mostly flat soda. "I don't know anything."

"They're good guys. They never meant for anything like this to happen—"

"Of course they didn't. Nobody ever means anything," I said.

"What?"

"Nothing."

Ryan stared at me for a second, then took a sip of soda. "They had no idea the water was going to be so rough. They didn't even know she was planning on jumping into the river when they went up there. I mean, you might not believe this, but it was her idea."

"No, I believe it."

"She kept saying how she was going to get a leap ahead on senior year, how she'd be a jump up on everyone else. She kept making stupid jokes like that."

"So you guys were jumping. Did you paint your initials first? Did she . . . "

Ryan nodded. "But I didn't go into the water. I mean, not until . . . she went, and then she didn't come up. I stopped a car and told them to call for help and then I dived in."

Suddenly I wanted to know the whole story—I couldn't stand not knowing anymore. "And then what?" I asked.

"You wouldn't believe how cold the river is right now. Maybe it was the snow—I don't know. It was like . . . so fast, too. By the time we found her, I . . . well, we did what we could. I mean, the thing is that she fought us. We were trying to pull her back up, to drag her to shore, but she was kicking Kevin and we couldn't . . . " Ryan's voice was wavering all over the place. I looked at him and his eyes were red and watery. "I've heard that's what happens sometimes. That's what my dad said, I think. It's a drowning phenomenon, how people panic and fight—"

"She wasn't panicking. Laurie didn't panic," I said. "Maybe she just didn't want you guys coming to her rescue. Maybe she was trying to get to shore on her own. Like that night in the rowboat when you came to get us and we were fine."

"No, it's a completely unconscious thing—a physical reaction," Ryan said.

"I don't think you know what you're talking about," I said.

"Alison, please. I'm sorry. I'm so sorry we all went out, and I'm sorry Laurie came and found us. And I'm sorry that when she dared those guys they said yeah, let's do it." He didn't say anything for a few minutes.

I took another sip of my soda and stared across the road. "Sorry" was still the most hollow-sounding word in the world.

"She was an original. There wasn't anyone else like her," Ryan said.

I wanted to hit him then. He didn't know Laurie. He had no idea what she was like. If he did, he would have asked her out, and not me, and she wouldn't have been there trying to prove something to everyone.

"So is there anything I can say or do? A bunch of us started a collection so we can get a memorial at school, and maybe something by the water, too—a plaque maybe—"

"What are you *doing*?" I glared at him.

"What?"

"What do you know about memorials? Are you in charge now, because you were *there*?" I said.

Ryan shifted in the chair. "I'm going to go now." He stood up and set his unopened can of soda on the porch railing. "See you around. Call me if you need anything." He stopped halfway to his pickup and turned around. "Alison, I know you hate me, but I really am sorry. And me and Kevin and Paul always will be, but you can hate us anyway. You probably should. I don't care."

I watched him drive away. I couldn't move from the porch for the longest time. The sun was going down, and I was getting cold, and I couldn't move. I was waiting for Sam and Dad to come back. I couldn't move from that spot. If I did, I wasn't sure what would happen, what I might do.

CHAPTER TWENTY-TWO

The memorial service was on Tuesday at 10:30 in the morning. Dad, Sam, and I didn't talk on the way to the church. I sat in the backseat, as usual—in my stupid black dress that still had the dry cleaners' plastic on it when I pulled it out of the back of my closet—and thought about the last time. Dad and Sam must have been thinking about it, too, but they were talking about the weather. It was raining, the kind of nice, light spring rain that made the ground smell earthy and brought out the flowers.

Last time, we had the memorial service on a Saturday and the St. Joseph's schedule had been so booked with September weddings that the memorial service had to be squeezed between two weddings. We had to be out of there before the next wedding party arrived, so we wouldn't cast a pall on the proceedings.

Then, at the memorial service, our dad decided to play host, standing by the entrance, greeting everyone who came into the church. I didn't understand what he was doing, why he was making small talk, why everyone was chatting and some even smiling and hugging. It was like he was avoiding me and Sam to mingle instead.

The worst part about the service was coming home afterward. It was hot and sunny. A nice early-September day. It didn't connect with what was happening. It should have been cold and gray and raining and windy. Instead, it was the kind of day we would usually spend outside, sitting on the porch together and reading or talking, then having a cookout and the four of us playing croquet in the backyard until it got too dark to see and even then we'd keep playing.

We weren't supposed to have a house full of strangers, with my dad asking me to circulate with a tray of cheese and crackers. I knew he was only trying to keep me busy, that he didn't know what to do with me. But it just felt like that same, bizarre, absurd thing when you were expected to pretend that everything was okay and it was okay for you to be offering people you didn't know cheese and crackers when it was the worst week of your entire life.

All those friends of hers from work that I didn't know, who stood in a circle around Mrs. K. My grandparents and cousins out on the porch. Sam playing basketball in the driveway with his friends, still wearing his dark suit. Everyone hanging around our house afterward, wanting to *do* something, talking incessantly, bringing us food. It was all so stupid. The only thing that made sense was when Laurie took the tray away from me and gave me a soda and made me go outside with her and plot our sophomore year.

• • •

At the church, we sat in the second pew, behind Mrs. Kuzmuskus and her sister, Laurie's aunt. Mrs. K. was wearing a black dress and a black hat with a veil over her face. My father put his hand on her shoulder as he sat down, and for some reason the way he did that made me feel faint, like it was too nice, too sweet.

Across the aisle, in the other front pew, was Mr. Kuzmuskus, by himself. I hadn't seen him in a long time. I didn't even really know him anymore. At least he had the sense not to have his new wife and their kids sit up there with him. Laurie would be happy about that.

The minister waited while the church filled to overflowing. Everyone from school was there. Everyone from the *Bugle*. All her teachers. Mr. Garcia and Mr. Lewis and Principal O'Neill. Even Kook, in that dark suit again, looking like an ape. I didn't see the Gods, but I thought that if they were here, then they were probably sitting in the back, hiding.

The minister talked for a while, and then he invited different people to come up and speak. Mrs. K. hadn't wanted it planned; when we got together to choose music and to paste photos onto poster board, she'd told me that anyone who wanted to speak, could. I knew she assumed I was going to say something, and I wanted to. I just didn't think that I could. And I didn't want to tell her that because I knew I'd be letting her down.

The first person to stand up was Mr. Garcia. On his

way past me, I noticed he was wearing the shoes that Laurie liked the best, the ones she always threatened to steal even though they'd be three sizes too big for her. "Every once in a while, a student comes along and changes things and changes the way you look at things," he said, and then I couldn't listen anymore—it was too hard. Mr. Lewis got up and actually praised Laurie for being a "free thinker," Mr. Lewis who was wearing his usual uncasual clothes and who looked gray and old all of a sudden.

The next person who got up was Kelley, which I couldn't believe. She and Laurie had never been friends, not really. I was jealous of her now, because she was up there and talking and I couldn't. I'd tried to work on a speech. But what was the point when I knew I wouldn't be able to read it out loud?

"Laurie was the driving force behind our best work," Kelley said, going on and on about Laurie and her writing, mentioning the award she'd won in Boston at the ceremony I hadn't gone to. Everything she said was true, and she even had a funny story about Laurie; and I couldn't stop thinking what Laurie would think of Kelley now, how she would critique her comments, what her comebacks would be.

When Kelley went back to her seat, Patrick got up. I noticed his father sitting there next to him. Patrick was carrying something in his right hand, but I couldn't see what it was. He started to say something, and a candy in his mouth clinked against his teeth and the microphone picked up the sound. If Laurie were here she would say something like, "Patrick Kirkpatrick, what the hell are you doing giving a speech and eating candy?" and "He'll kill you if he catches you with candy," and suddenly I was back in geometry, with her and Patrick, that first day, when he asked about hyperteneuse triangles and we both realized he didn't have a clue.

"The thing is, when something tragic and horrible like this happens, you can't help asking, you know," Patrick began, "the proverbial question. The important question. The question Laurie was always asking us. Which is . . . Kuz why?"

There were a few laughs, smiles, nods of recognition in the crowd. I guess it made everyone happy to remember. It made me even more miserable.

Hearing Patrick's voice made me remember the good things but also how I'd deliberately hurt Laurie, how I'd told her Patrick was only with her because I wasn't. Why did I have to do that? What was wrong with me?

"'Cause why?" Patrick repeated. "Why does something this horrible have to happen? 'Cause it makes no sense. 'Cause it's wrong and stupid to lose someone as great as Laurie." He looked out at the crowd. His eyes met mine and he quickly looked down at his speech again. "You know, the first time I met Laurie was in geometry. Her best subject and my worst." He glanced out in the direction of Mr. Lewis. "But she made it easy for me from the beginning.

234

She made fun of me, sure. She teased me constantly. But then she was only being herself. Which was why she was such a good friend. When I got here, she made me feel like I belonged. She never hesitated to make a joke about anything or anyone. But at the same time she always wanted to protect people, to make other people like me feel better. Even about failing geometry. So why is that the person we have to lose?" He took a deep breath and his voice was rough when he spoke again.

"'Cause why?" Patrick said. "'Cause I said so, that's why. Kuzmustkiss, we're going to miss you." He walked over and drew his hand out from behind his back and that's when I saw it, the green plastic hat, the one she'd given him on St. Patrick's Day, the one he wore that night at the party when we were all dancing together, back before everything got so messed up and complicated. Patrick placed the hat carefully on top of the casket.

On his way back to his seat, Patrick stopped beside me. Don't stop, I thought. Keep going.

Then he crouched down and hugged me and I felt my arms just hanging at my sides, totally limp. I couldn't hug him back. He was pulling me closer and closer and I could smell the candy in his mouth, and I heard Laurie saying, 'What's that smell, sour something?' as Patrick let me go and leaned back on his heels, pushing a few strands of my hair off my face, strands that came out of my silver barrette the way they always did.

Patrick kissed me on the cheek and walked away, and I felt like my chest was being forced open, cracked open, split down the middle. I couldn't breathe right. I couldn't get any air. The minister was waiting for the next person to go talk, and it should be me, I should be able to go up there and say something. I should tell them all the incredible and wonderful things about Laurie. I could go on and on. I knew more than anyone. I knew her better than anyone. But I couldn't open my mouth. I couldn't do it.

I stood up and my father said, "Alison, good for you," because he thought I was getting up to talk, and everyone was looking at me, waiting for me to go up to the pulpit and say something, and I pushed my way out of the pew and ran out of the church.

There were already bouquets of flowers lying at the spot, in the middle of the bridge. Some wrapped in cellophane, some looking like they'd been pulled from a town park. I looked down at the river, a light mist rising from it and mixing with the soft rain falling from the sky.

Even though I was a better swimmer, even though I knew how, I could never jump from here. It was the unknown—the water was opaque and unforgiving. What would it feel like? I wondered. My eyes watered from the breeze. I couldn't imagine jumping, now that I was standing here and really thinking about it, picturing it. I wished that I could, but who was I kidding? Of course I couldn't.

Why hadn't I known that, why hadn't I realized that by now? Laurie was brave; she took risks. I didn't. She wasn't afraid of anything; I was afraid of everything.

This wasn't happening like the last time, but everything felt exactly the same.

I hadn't heard while standing at my locker.

It hadn't been an illness that shocked us but at the same time let us know when we had to say good-bye.

This time there was no chance to say good-bye. There was no chance to take back the things I'd said.

Not looking at pictures for the past six months hadn't helped.

Not remembering didn't help.

Nothing helped. Nothing protected you. Nothing stopped it from coming and nothing stopped it from happening again.

You think you have it figured out, Patrick had said to me. *You don't know anything.*

I stood on the bridge looking down at the river beneath me. It was impossible to think about, to imagine. At the same time, I could see her so clearly, could see her long hair streaming out as she flung herself off the side after Kevin, like the way her hair flew behind her when we rode our bikes to the launch. She would have been laughing and shouting, "Chicken!" over her shoulder to Ryan and she wouldn't have been ready to hit the water, her mouth would still be open and she'd gulp in a mouthful of dirty river water and try to come up gasping for air.

Why is it named for a king? It ought to be a prince or a duke—you can't name a pond for a king; it has to be something big, like a sea or an ocean.

I don't know how long I was standing there. But suddenly there was a long line of cars, all with their headlights on, coming across the bridge. At first I thought it was because of the rain but as they got closer, I saw the little orange flags on their antennas. And then I realized it was them—it was Mrs. K. in the second car, it was Laurie in the first, which was the hearse. They were on the way to the cemetery.

Everyone else would see me standing there—they were staring out their windows at me, wondering what I was going to do next. And then they slowed down, and they were creeping by, and then they were stopped. The hearse was going ahead because that driver didn't know me, but everyone else was motionless; and I wondered how the bridge would support all those cars and I wondered if Patrick was in one of them and whether being up here was making him nervous.

And then Sam was running down the sidewalk to me, his black wingtip shoes clicking against the wet pavement, and he was standing beside me, and all the cars were moving on. He looked so grown-up in his suit. He'd never had a nice suit before, and now he'd had to wear it twice in one year.

"Don't," he said, out of breath when he stopped. "You won't."

I shook my head slowly. "No, I wasn't going to."

"You're sure?" he said.

"Yes." I wasn't completely sure, but I had to tell him that I was.

"Promise me."

"I can't promise anything, Sam—"

"No. *Promise* me!" And he was yelling at me and grabbing my arms like he'd done that day at the bowling alley.

I nodded. "Okay."

And then he let me go. He pulled the carnation off his suit jacket and dropped it into the river, then ran to the other side of the bridge to see it go past, to test the current, like we always used to do when we were kids.

Then we walked down to meet Dad, who was waiting in the car at the end of the bridge, pulled over at the scenic overlook, with the emergency flashers on.

CHAPTER TWENTY-THREE

My father drove me to school the next day, the first day we all went back. On the way, at first I closed my eyes so I wouldn't see the falls and the flowers, so I wouldn't have to remember.

Then I opened them. Avoiding things didn't work. It had never worked. It didn't keep me from losing Laurie. It didn't keep me from remembering bad things.

I had to keep reminding myself that there was no point having rules. Rules hadn't saved me from anything.

So I opened my eyes when we went past Riverbank Paper and I stared at everyone filing into work.

When I got to school, there was this giant poster board with pictures of Laurie tacked onto it and cards and messages and teddy bears and flowers. There was a table where Kook and extra counselors were sitting, waiting for us. Principal O'Neill was there, too, greeting people and trying to let everyone know how much she cared.

I kept thinking how Laurie would have just made fun of all of this, but then, maybe not. We hadn't lost a classmate before. This was new.

I knew that people were talking about what had happened, analyzing it, and that everyone was looking at me again, wondering how I was doing, feeling sorry for me and wondering when I was going to crack. I was the butterfly again. Pinned up. I'd never been in this school without Laurie. All I could think was I'm not going into Kook's office again, I'm not. If he summons me, I'm not going. I'll leave.

I put my head down and walked past him and the others. I didn't even know what I was doing here, just that my dad thought it was a good idea, and I'd sort of been clinging to him since that night, doing whatever he said. It was easier that way, not to make my own decisions. And, besides, for the first time in a while, I trusted him. I had no other choice.

Squeak, squeak. I heard footsteps behind me, and I glanced over my shoulder. And there was Kook in a red sweatsuit, following me down the hall, keeping a respectable distance but still following me, his long arms hanging at his sides, his sneakers squeaking on the freshly waxed floor.

I did the only thing I could think of to get him to leave me alone. I turned down a hall I never went down, the one that smelled like simmering beakers and sulfur and explosions. I ran my hand along the wall, skimming the numbers, counting down. At 158 I stopped. My heart was pounding.

Oh, god, what was I doing here? I couldn't do this.

I couldn't remember the combination at first. I heard Kook's footsteps and I started racing to open it, like a robber at a bank safe when the alarms are going off and the police are en route. Right to 15, left 4, right 36.

When I popped it open, dozens of scraps of paper fell out onto the floor. I ignored them for a second and stared at the photos on the inside of the door—me and Laurie, me and Laurie and our moms—and at the stickers for different bands, bands I didn't even listen to anymore. There was a card with a haircut appointment taped to the door, an appointment from last September, my back-to-school trim that I'd canceled or probably just never shown up for.

There were notes jammed onto the locker's top shelf and some notes still stuck in the grate. I reached down and picked up a yellow scrap from the floor. It said:

> *Alison—Today is the anniversary of the day the Gods from Mt. Vesuvius awoke and noticed us. Well, not us. You. March 3. Don't forget it. Ever.*

My eyes watered as I picked up another note. Then another and another. They were all from Laurie. She'd been leaving me notes almost every day since then.

> *We got cut from soccer today. To add insult to injury, it's Fish Stick Friday. Hate Coach Crandall. Hate her. Must go leave fish sticks in her locker now. Not sure they will fit through slots, though.*

Only 90 days until summer vacation. Then what? I don't know. But we won't be sophomores anymore.

People were walking by me in the hallway and the notes started blowing around the hall. I sat down and scraped them all into a heap with my arms. They were all lying there in a heap now, on pink, green, and yellow paper, like giant confetti.

Dear Miss Pimpalicious,
You are a disco queen. Dancing queen. Whatever.
We should have parties more often, no?
Or at least Patrick should.

Remember when we went through that shoplifting phase in 7th grade? How stupid were we? Not only was it wrong, but we were horrible at it. Sort of like dieting. Pointless.

kuz why does Patrick have to be so good-looking? Is he trying to torment me?

We will look back on all this someday and laugh. However, I think we can start laughing now. kuz if we don't, we'll probably start weeping.

Patrick Fitzpatrick = major improvement in social life. Spatially challenged, however. A bit obtuse. Do not ask him to pack a box for you, ever.

Here are the reject proofs from picture day. Please destroy as necessary.

I sorted through the stack of paper on the floor, looking for the proofs. When I found them and pulled the sheet of pictures out of the pile and saw Laurie's face, I burst into tears. I sat there on the floor, staring at the photos, crying, not even caring that I was in the middle of the hall, that people were showing up for chem lab, that Kook must still be nearby somewhere, hovering, crouching in a wrestler's pose. Through my blurred eyes I could see feet going past, different shoes and boots and sneakers. Some people were ignoring me and some pausing, then moving on, leaving me. I brushed my eyes with my sleeve and picked up another note, but I could hardly read it, and now tears were falling onto the notes. I took a deep breath and searched inside my backpack for a tissue but couldn't find one, so I used my jacket sleeve to wipe my eyes and kept reading.

So this really embarrassing thing just happened that I didn't even tell you about. I came out of the bathroom with TP stuck to

my shoe and guess who was standing there.
Mr. Garcia. And he said, "Um, Laurie, you, um,"
which made it ten times worse. His shoes are
so cool that TP doesn't even stick to them.

I know you're not really using your locker now,
but what the heck. At the end of the school
year, they'll make you clean it out. Which is a
good thing because I think it's starting to smell
funny. Did you leave a sandwich in here last
year?

The Bungle is going to win major awards. Call
me when it happens.

And then there was a typed note on official Birch Falls
Regional High School stationery:

```
Alison,
Please stop by my office when you have a
chance.
Perhaps Tuesday during lunch.
I thought we could talk.
Thank you.
Mr. Cucklowicz
```

And another, as I sorted through the stack of notes:

Alison,

Haven't heard from you.

Wondering if everything is all right.

Please come by.

Mr. Cucklowicz

And then more from Laurie:

Even though we're fighting now, I'm still leaving notes. I must be insane or something. I prefer "or something," if anyone asks. Less stigma attached.

And then, on a typed note that fell from the top shelf, on school stationery:

Alison,

I've cleared my schedule for you.

You rock my world.

Lovingly,

Kook

P.S. This note typed by psycho secretary L. Kuzmuskus

I started laughing hysterically, and I saw Kook perched at the end of the hall, still watching me and wondering why

I was laughing so hard. Which made me laugh even more, but at the same time I was still crying. I was a mess.

I made as much of a neat, orderly stack of the notes as I could, which was sort of impossible because they were all different shapes and sizes and several were quite crumpled. I put most of them into my bag, except for a couple that I put into my pocket to read again, to keep close to me. I could take the rest of them home and read them later. Maybe I'd make a collage out of them for my bedroom wall.

Then I took the books I needed for my morning classes out of my bag and left it inside the locker. I'd missed my first class, but I could get there for the second.

After school on Friday, I went home to call Dad, to tell him I was all right. Then I rode my bike over to Patrick's house. He was outside, by the garage, working on a bicycle that was hanging from a pole.

He slowly smiled when he realized it was me riding up the driveway toward him. "Hey."

"Hi." I leaned the bike against the side of the garage. "What's going on?"

"Not much. I was about to go for a ride."

"Oh. Well, don't let me stop you."

"I won't," he said. He laughed nervously. "That sounded rude. Sorry. I just meant . . . it's daylight savings time now. So I have time."

"Okay." I wandered around the backyard. "You have a

really nice view from up here. Across the valley."

"Yeah. Dad insisted on it when he was house hunting. I guess this way he can see if the factory's on fire or something."

"I think we could *all* see that," I said. "Or smell it, anyway."

"Probably," Patrick agreed. "Yeah. You know, small-town life . . . it's different, you know? It takes some adjusting."

"How so?"

"Well, everyone knows everyone else. Which can be sort of annoying at times, like you can't get away with anything. But, then, when something bad happens, it's kind of a good thing."

"I guess," I said. Sometimes I was still trying to decide whether that was a good thing or not. "You . . . you gave a really nice speech. The other day."

"Oh. You think so?" Patrick asked. I nodded. "Good. I mean, not that I was doing it to hear that. I stayed up all night trying to write something that didn't sound . . . *canned*. You know. Like what anyone else would say. It had to be original, because . . . well, you know why."

"You did a good job," I said. "So. Remember that day when you said maybe you wouldn't be here for senior year? You're not leaving, are you?"

"No. I'm going to try not to, anyway. My dad and I are getting along okay these days, so as long as I can stay away from the bags of frozen vegetables and actually pass geometry—did I tell you Mr. Lewis is tutoring me? Personally? Every day during study hall. When Laurie tried, I could never concentrate. I just wanted to joke around. So, my dad says, if I quit the *Bugle*—"

"Don't quit the *Bugle*!" I said quickly.

"Why not? You did."

I shrugged. "True." Then I took a deep breath. I had to apologize to him. I had to try to explain why I'd pushed him away and how much I'd regretted it but how I couldn't have done anything else. "You know, Patrick? I'm sorry," I said. "I'm sorry I was so stupid about everything. That day you came over."

"No. It's my fault," Patrick said.

"No! It was mine. I liked you. I mean—not past tense and everything—I still do, but I couldn't . . . I just wasn't ready. Or I didn't know how I was supposed to be ready," I said. "Like this really good thing was happening, and it was all messed up. Because I didn't deserve it. Because I just feel sort of guilty when I'm doing okay." I looked over at him.

"You have to do okay eventually," he said. "That's sort of the deal."

"I guess. Do you understand, though?"

"Yeah." He looked at my bike. "So. Are you finally bringing that in for repairs?"

"No, I wasn't planning on it," I said. "It still works."

"Sure, it works, if you want to wear earplugs. Hold on." Patrick went into the garage and sorted through his bikes, all leaning against the wall. He came out with a red bike that had orange lettering on it. "I think this one would fit you. Let's adjust the seat and then you can ride it home."

"That's okay. I don't need it," I said.

"Come on, take it. It's my C bike."

"But . . . that's your third best. Right? I don't want to take it," I said.

"Look. Leave your old one here and I'll fix it. But if it can't be fixed, or you like this one better, then we can just trade. Okay?" Patrick was insistent.

After a few adjustments, I was sitting comfortably on the new bike. "I have to get going. I promised Mrs. Kuzmuskus I'd drop by, and there are some other places I want to go, too."

"I can go with you," Patrick said.

"No. You're going on your training ride, and—"

"That's not important."

"Yeah. But I should probably . . . I should do it myself," I said.

"Oh. Okay. So, see you around?" Patrick asked.

I nodded, smiled at him, and then rode away. I was going on a tour. Every place that we hung out together, every place we liked to go, even those we didn't. I rode down to the launch, wishing I could crash into Laurie at the bottom of the hill. If we'd only crashed, everything would have turned out differently—we would have been injured, maybe we wouldn't have been able to go to Boston, maybe we never would have fought. At the launch, I looked at the aluminum rowboat still lying under that tree and thought about our disastrous boat ride and about the night we first came here freshman year and how excited we were that the Gods had invited us.

I left the launch and rode over the bridge to downtown, over the narrow canal bridges. I rode past Frenchy's Candy Kitchen and then on to school and across the soccer field where we'd tried out and failed, and then down to Salvage City and the paper factory. The shifts were changing at the factory and I watched everyone stream out to their cars with their empty lunch bags and coolers; and then there were the people that split off from the group and they didn't go to their cars, they went straight to Jerry's Tavern.

I didn't have a bike lock with me, and I didn't want to chance having Patrick's bike stolen, so I couldn't go inside. But I stood there and watched other people going in, talking and laughing. I pictured my mother and Mrs. K. hurrying over on a Friday afternoon after work with the rest of their coworkers. Then I pictured Sam walking in with her on a Wednesday afternoon, and started to cry. She should still be here, she should still be able to do this, I thought. It wasn't fair that she couldn't, it wasn't fair that they were still here and she wasn't. But neither was trying to forget she used to be. I wouldn't do that anymore.

• • •

When I got home, I went up to my room and stared at the jumbled heap of Laurie's notes on my desk. I didn't know what to do with them all. I needed to do something, though.

I pulled the shoebox off the top shelf in the closet. I stacked the notes as neatly as I could, into a pile about two inches thick. Then I looked at the box. I'd put that stuff away because it made me cry. Then there were times I looked at it and I couldn't cry, which felt even worse.

I lifted up the lid, ready to push the notes down on top of the pictures. But then I stopped and hesitated for a second. I reached into the middle of the stack. I pulled out a picture, which was upside down.

I flipped the photo over and stared at it. It was the four of us: me and Laurie, about ten years old, both with our long hair, standing back to back to see whose was longest—and Mom and Mrs. K. standing behind us, holding scissors, threatening to cut it off.

A week ago Laurie had stood here and told me to start living, to put up a calendar at least.

I stuck the picture back onto the big, empty bulletin board. Then I sifted through the stack of notes and found one of my favorite ones and put it up next to the picture.

"Alison? You okay?" Dad knocked lightly on the door and poked his head in. "We're going out—you know, our Friday night routine, so—" He stopped. "Sorry."

"It's okay," I said. "You didn't think."

"No, I didn't. I should work on that." Dad gently banged his head against the side of the doorway. He glanced at the shoebox, at the pile of notes. "Anyway, you want to come along? Do you want to go out or stay in . . . whatever you want."

"Let's go out," I said. I could only take so much of this at a time.

CHAPTER TWENTY-FOUR

When I got up on Saturday morning, I called Mrs. K. It was only eight o'clock and I was pretty sure I'd be waking her up. Then again, she probably wasn't sleeping all that well these days, so maybe not. As the phone was ringing on her end, I opened the cabinet above the toaster and started looking.

When she answered the phone, her voice was gravelly and low. "Hello?" She sounded as if she did not want to be called.

"Hey, Mrs. K. It's me," I said.

"Alison? What's wrong?" Her voice was raspy, as if she'd smoked herself hoarse overnight.

"Nothing. Nothing's wrong!" Except the usual, I thought. Which we both know and both know we can't talk about. "I was just wondering. Do you want to come over for pancakes?" I pulled a box of pancake mix out of the back of the cabinet.

"What?"

"I'm making pancakes. Blueberry, if you're lucky," I said as I walked to the refrigerator to check for frozen fruit.

"Alison?" Her voice shook now, like she was crying.

"It's me, Mrs. K. Come on, come over."

"I'm not even awake yet."

"I know. But get yourself in the shower and get over here," I said. I sounded just like Laurie. I guess in some ways I was pretending I was her. I didn't know how to do this myself, so I was doing what she would have done. What she did for me, for my family, afterward.

"I guess I could," she said.

"I'm giving you twenty minutes. I'm starting the coffeemaker now."

Mrs. K. coughed a few times. "Alison? Is everything okay?"

"No, but what else is new," I said. "Just come over. Please?"

When my dad came into the kitchen to see what I was doing, I asked, "Do you think you could make coffee? I'm not as good at it as you are."

"Sure, but . . . what's going on?"

I dumped the box of breakfast sausages into one of the frying pans. "I'm making breakfast. I want to get Mrs. Kuzmuskus over here." I got out a measuring cup and started filling it with pancake mix.

"You what?" my dad asked.

"I just don't think she should be alone right now," I said. I checked the back of the mix box, looking for the amount of water and eggs I needed to add. Laurie always did this, while I sat at the counter and watched.

"No," my father said. He opened a drawer and took out a coffee filter. "You're right, she shouldn't."

"Especially not on the weekends. Those are the hardest," I said as I stirred the batter.

He didn't say anything, but I knew he knew what I meant. It was like we were all gritting our teeth to get through the day. Sam was once again glued to the television, watching extreme sports and cartoons, eating out of the latest box of no-name cereal from Salvage City. I was starting to be more worried about him.

"Hey, if you want to get Mrs. K. out of the house . . . or whatever," Sam said over his shoulder. Then he got up and came into the kitchen to get a glass of orange juice. "I mean, I don't know how her bowling game is, but maybe we could play teams on Sunday."

"I don't think she likes bowling any more than Laurie does," I said. Did. Any more than Laurie did. I looked at the refrigerator as my eyes filled with tears.

Sam covered for me. "Hey, maybe she likes really bad nachos. Or she could always come just to laugh at me." He filled his glass and placed the carton of orange juice back on the counter. "Forty-three. Who goes bowling once a week and still gets a forty-three? Why can I do any other sport except bowling?"

"Maybe it's like me and geometry," I said. "It's a mental block."

"It's genetic or something, you mean?" Sam said. "Okay,

cool. Then that's the excuse I'm using from now on."

"So, um, what do you want to do today, Alison?" my dad asked. "Any plans?"

"No. Not really," I said. No, not at all, I thought. Because Laurie's not here anymore and I have no clue how to spend my time. "Maybe I'll go to that baseball tournament with you. What time would we leave?"

"The game's at two, so . . . noon?" Dad smiled.

"Ask Patrick to come," Sam added. "Tell him there's going to be speed pitching."

After breakfast, after Sam cleared away the dishes and while Dad was cleaning up the kitchen, Mrs. K. and I went outside onto the porch. I was worried about Mrs. K. She didn't look too good. She didn't look like herself, even. And she'd barely talked at all.

We stood on the top step for a minute. "Do you want to come with us? To the baseball game this afternoon?" I asked.

She shook her head. "No. No, thanks."

"Are you sure?" I asked. I didn't know whether I was asking for her sake or for mine. At least when she was around I could still feel close to Laurie, but at the same time there was an obvious gap where she was supposed to be standing, because Mrs. K. and I never just did something together without her, unless it was shopping for Laurie's birthday present.

"It's okay, Alison," Mrs. K. finally said. She leaned

against the porch railing and sighed.

"It is?" I asked, perching on the railing beside her.

"No. But my sister's coming up today—she'll be there when I get home. Actually, she might be moving in with me for a while."

"Oh, yeah? Well, that sounds . . . good. I guess."

She nodded. "Yeah. I can't really . . . be there by myself. You know."

"Yeah. I—I couldn't either," I said.

"I should probably move." Mrs. K. took a pack of cigarettes out of her purse and shook one out. But she didn't light it. She just kept tapping it against the heel of her palm. "What next? You know, Alison? I mean, I don't know how I'm going to go on."

I tried to think of something to say, something that would make sense and wouldn't sound fake and phony, like a drugstore card. Something better than "sorry." I wondered if she knew how I'd broken down at school, if that was the kind of thing Kook told parents, who then told their friends. Maybe everyone in town knew by now. I wouldn't care if they did.

"I found some things in my locker—from Laurie. Some notes she left me," I finally said. "I thought maybe you'd want some of them. I can bring them over next week sometime."

"No, you keep them," Mrs. K. said, shaking her head. "I have lots of things—cards and . . . you know. But maybe there are other things you want to take. Clothes or something? I don't know."

"Sure, okay." I tried to imagine what I would take, what I would want. Her old typewriter, the one she insisted on writing her columns on. The hat from the night of Patrick's party, the one with the feather. That beat-up Salvage City leather jacket.

"Do you think maybe? Do you think you could go with me sometime? To the cemetery?" Mrs. K. asked.

"I . . . " I couldn't stand the thought of it. I hadn't gotten out of the car during Laurie's burial, but if Mrs. K. wanted me to go with her, I would. I'd have to. I nodded. "Okay."

"You haven't been there. That's what Laurie said. Not since—"

"No," I said, swallowing hard. "Not since her birthday." That was the day I decided there was no point going back to old places that made me crumble inside. Because I had to stop crumbling or I'd fall apart completely and I couldn't do that. I hadn't been to the cemetery in a long time, but I hadn't forgotten the way to my mother's grave. I knew exactly where it was, which dirt path to take.

"We'll go together. Don't go unless I go with you," Mrs. K. said.

And I smiled, because that was something that Laurie always used to say. "Mrs. K.? Laurie wasn't trying to . . . I mean, she never thought. That she wouldn't make it. She wasn't trying to leave you."

Mrs. K. nodded. "I know. At least I think I know."

We walked over to her car then, and even though I knew I'd see her tomorrow and that I was going to stop by her house every day for a while, I gave her a hug good-bye. Then we stood by the Sundance awkwardly. "Call me anytime," I said. "I mean it. Okay?"

Mrs. K. nodded. "Will do."

On Sunday Patrick was waiting for me on the steps to the second floor of Salvage City, like we'd planned. "Check it out. Look what I found." He held up two bowling balls; one purple and one green.

"But those are huge. They're for regular bowling, not candlepin," I said.

"Yeah, but think how badly we can beat Sam now," he said. "Huh? Huh? Brilliant or what?"

"Rick would ban us for life if we tried it." I took the purple swirl bowling ball from him and held it up to the light. "I don't think this is round. Is it?"

"Yeah. Well, there is that. The whole oval thing could be a challenge." Patrick laughed, as he tried to jam his fingers into the holes, which weren't quite big enough. I was laughing, watching him. Then I felt so guilty, because how could I still be here, joking around with Patrick, when they were both gone? How was I supposed to just go on with my life? But what else could I do? I had stopped my life for a while, and that didn't work, either.

"So Kelley called me this morning," Patrick said as we started wandering around the store. I didn't know where I was going, but it felt better to keep moving somehow. "You won't believe this, but she wants to do a special issue in honor of Laurie."

"She does?" I said. "You know what? It won't be any fun to do it . . . to do the paper. Without . . . her," I said. I forced the words out. "Without Laurie." And then I started crying. I was crying, in the middle of Salvage City, next to the bargain candy. This was the worst. This was worse than at school, even. There wasn't a rule about this posted on the door but there should be: No Crying in Aisle 12. "Sorry. I don't usually do this."

"It's all the smoke in the air," Patrick said, moving a little closer to me. He was trying to cover for me, and I sort of loved him for it. "No, it won't be any fun doing the *High Bugle* without her. It'll be horrible. Everything's going to be horrible. For a long time." He put his arms around me and hugged me. He ran his hand along the top of my head, following my hair, playing with the end of my ponytail. "God, do I know how to make someone feel better or what? I suck at this."

"No, you don't," I said. "I do."

I hugged him back, and we just stood like that for a minute, until the curvy smock-topped clerk, still wearing her "I'm New Here!" button, tried to get past us in the aisle.

She couldn't fit past us, and she sort of nudged me with her curvy hips. "Excuse me. Coming through."

Patrick and I stepped apart awkwardly, leaning back toward a bin of overstock spice drops so that she could go by us. "Come on. Let's go bowling."

"I don't even like bowling that much," I told him.

"I know. Neither do I," Patrick said. "But what else are we going to do?"

CHAPTER TWENTY-FIVE

In geometry class, Mr. Lewis was leaving Laurie's desk empty. Even he couldn't rearrange the legendary, accurate seating chart so that he got rid of her space. He'd even given up his alternate Monday quizzes. It was like we were all just coasting, hoping we had enough to make it to the end of the year.

It had been a month, and life wasn't getting back to normal, for anyone. Least of all for me. I felt like I was still numb sometimes. And other times, I was the complete opposite, crying while I ate breakfast or whenever I saw something that reminded me of her—or of my mother. Which was everything, really, but sometimes it made me happy to remember and sometimes absolutely miserable.

But I was talking to people about it—about them—now. I was writing in that blank book that I'd carried around for months. Nothing as good as what Laurie would have written, nothing witty or clever. But words on the page. I was writing as much as I could, it seemed like.

I even sat in geometry class that Friday morning in May

and wrote notes. I knew Mr. Lewis would forgive me. Nobody wanted to push us right now. He'd have to pull it together and give us a final—and I'd have to study enough to pass it—but he wasn't making much effort right now.

Patrick looked over at my desk and probably wondered what I was doing, how I could write so much, use so many pages when all we were supposed to be doing was problems from our textbook.

At lunchtime, I rode my bike down to the bridge. There were even more flowers threaded through the railing now—real ones and plastic bouquets. There were plastic-covered photos of Laurie pinned to the metal railing and cards whose ink had run in the rain.

I posted my note next to them on the bridge.

So guess what?
Fish Stick Friday has finally been canceled due to student complaints. Maybe it was your endless columns about it. Or maybe it was Saint Patrick, driving them out of town. So get this. They're replacing it with Fish Filet Friday, starting today.
As if we don't know it's practically the same thing.
I'm skipping, in protest. For you.
P.S. More tomorrow.

DATE DUE

GAYLORD   #3523PI   Printed in USA